THE WORDS OF US

MARGAUX FOX

PROLOGUE

I sit slouched in one of those uncomfortable airport chairs, one leg tucked beneath me, the other tapping against the floor in rhythm with my restless thoughts. The noise around me is the usual airport chaos—flight announcements, people rushing past—but somehow, it feels like I'm standing still in the middle of it all.

My backpack, faded and beaten up from too many trips, is slumped next to me. It's barely filled, just a few things inside, but it feels heavy—like it's carrying more than just my belongings. I pick at the frayed edges of my hoodie sleeve, glancing out the huge windows where planes take off and land without a care that mine isn't going anywhere yet.

I can see my reflection in the glass: dark hair tied back in a messy knot, pieces slipping out to frame my tired face. My eyes look older than they should, like they've seen too much, though I'm dressed simply in jeans, a t-shirt, and a pair of sneakers that have been through hell with me. No makeup, no jewelry—just the basics.

Inside my backpack, there's not much: a notebook, a single pen, and a dog-eared book of poems I can't seem to let go of. I don't need a lot. I'm traveling light on purpose, leaving behind what doesn't fit, what I can't carry with me anymore.

The crackle of the loudspeaker makes me wince, and I already know what's coming before the announcement even finishes. "Flight 322 to New Orleans has been delayed by an additional two hours." The words hang in the air like a lead weight. I let out an audible sigh, slumping further into the chair as frustration bubbles up inside me. Great. Just what I needed. More time in this limbo, stuck here when all I want is to be anywhere else.

I rub my face, trying to will away the tiredness creeping in from hours of waiting. My eyes feel heavy, my patience worn thin. I shift in my seat, staring down at my worn sneakers, counting the flecks of dirt like they might offer me some comfort. They don't.

Suddenly, someone drops into the seat beside me. I glance over out of reflex and find myself looking at a woman. A total stranger. She's about my age, maybe a little older. Dressed casually with her hair pulled back in a loose braid, she looks just as tired as I feel, though she smiles faintly at me, like she's trying to make the best of this miserable situation.

"Long day?" she asks, her voice soft but friendly.

I can't help but let out a short, humorless laugh. "You could say that," I mutter, turning back toward the window.

I don't really feel like talking, not to her, not to anyone. But for some reason, I don't get up and leave either. Maybe because I'm too tired to move, or maybe because her presence is oddly calming. It's strange how just having someone sit beside you, even a stranger, can make the waiting feel a little less unbearable.

She doesn't push me to talk, and I'm grateful for that. We

sit there in silence, two tired souls stuck in the same nowhere place, waiting for the next thing, whatever that is. I close my eyes for a moment, letting the sounds of the airport fade into the background, and wonder what I'll do with all this extra time.

I sit up a bit straighter as I try to shake off the frustration. The woman beside me glances over, a smile pulling at the corners of her lips like she's seen this all before. She waits a beat before speaking, her voice low and warm.

"Days are just stories, you know," she says, her eyes fixed somewhere ahead, almost like she's talking to the air. "It's up to us how we tell them."

I blink, surprised by the unexpected wisdom in her words. I wasn't expecting that from a stranger in an airport, but there it is—simple yet somehow profound. I find myself chewing on the thought, letting it settle into the corners of my mind. *Days are just stories. Stories I can shape.* The idea twists inside me, softening the edges of my frustration just a little.

She turns her head, her gaze settling on me with a soft curiosity. "Tell me your story," she says gently.

I pause, caught off guard by the question. My story? The words don't come easily. I think about the last few years—about the pain, the problems, the running, all the things I've faced that feel too big and too tangled to put into words. The memories surge like a tide: the broken relationships, the sleepless nights, the moments when everything felt like it was falling apart.

I start to speak, stumbling over the words, my voice faltering under the weight of it all. But before I can get too far, she lifts her hand to stop me.

"See," she says, "I'm asking for *your* story. Tell it how you want. Rewrite it. I'm a stranger. You can tell it to me any way you want, and that's all I will know."

Her words hit me like a spark, igniting something inside. Rewrite it. Just like that. As if it's that simple. I look at her, trying to figure out if she's serious, but she is. And for a moment, the idea of rewriting my story—not just telling the past but shaping it, choosing what to hold on to and what to let go of—feels almost...possible.

I sit back in the chair, thinking it over. Maybe, just maybe, she's right. Maybe it's time to tell the story differently.

She doesn't push. She just sits there, watching the busy terminal like she has all the time in the world. There's a peaceful patience about her, like she knows exactly when to speak and when to let the silence do the work. And it does work. The longer the quiet stretches between us, the more her words start to sink in.

Rewrite it.

Finally, after what feels like an eternity, she turns to me again. "Tell me your story," she repeats, her voice gentle but insistent. There's no pressure in it, just a soft invitation.

I swallow hard, glancing down at my hands. I can feel the weight of her question pressing against my chest, but this time, it's different. She's not asking for the version I've been telling myself—the one filled with pain and mistakes. She's asking for *my* story, the one I want to tell.

I hesitate for just a second longer, then take a deep breath. Maybe it doesn't have to be so hard. Maybe, for once, I can choose what to say, and let everything else fade into the background.

I look up, meeting her eyes. "My story," I begin, this time more steady, "is still being written. But it started in a small suburb in New York—Westchester, actually." I pause, feeling the memories tug at me, but I choose to let the lighter ones come forward. "It was the kind of place where you could hear the ice cream truck two streets over in the summer, where everyone knew everyone. My childhood was...safe, I guess. Familiar."

I glance at the woman beside me. She's watching me with an encouraging smile, like she's waiting for me to find the rhythm. And I do. The words start to come a little easier now.

"But, you know, safety has a way of feeling small after a while. I wanted more. I craved something bigger, something louder. So I started writing poetry in high school—scribbling lines in the margins of my notebooks and performing at open mics whenever I could sneak away from suburbia. It became my way out, my escape hatch into a world that was wider and filled with possibilities."

I can feel the energy shifting inside me, the words flowing more naturally. I sit up a little straighter, feeling the pulse of something more vibrant, more alive.

"After college, I moved to the city for a while. Manhattan. It was thrilling, overwhelming, and everything I'd hoped for and more. But life has a way of shifting on you, you know? What starts out as a dream sometimes twists into something else. I got a little lost in it, in the noise, in the pressure to always be 'on.' I kept running, trying to find the right place, the right people, but nothing really stuck. It was like I was chasing shadows."

I stop for a breath, a small smile tugging at my lips as I think about where I'm heading next.

"And now... Now I'm heading to New Orleans. Not just for a fresh start but because I think it's where I'm supposed to be. It feels right, like there's something waiting for me there. I don't know exactly what it is yet, but I'm ready for it. Ready to let the next chapter write itself one day at a time."

I glance over at her, feeling lighter somehow, as if saying it out loud has made it more real. She nods slowly, her smile deepening as if she's pleased with what I've shared.

"Well," she says softly, "sounds like you've got quite a story ahead of you."

"Let's hope it is a good one." I smile.

The airport intercom crackles. "Flight 322 to New Orleans is now available for boarding."

1

EVIE

I stand in line at the small coffee shop just down the street from the bookstore, glancing at the chalkboard menu like I haven't already memorized it. The rich smell of freshly ground beans and warm pastries fills the air, and for a moment, I let it wrap around me like an old blanket, familiar and comforting.

My hair, a deep chestnut brown, is tied up in a loose bun that's already starting to come undone from the humid New Orleans air. Stray strands brush against my face, and I tuck them behind my ear absentmindedly. I'm dressed in my usual—an oversized sweater that drapes over my frame and a pair of worn-in jeans, comfortable and practical for long days spent shelving books and greeting customers. My skin, sun-kissed from years of walking the streets of this city, has a soft warmth to it, and the faintest lines around my eyes show more laughter than anything else.

"Evie?" the barista calls.

I step forward, wrapping my hands around the warm paper cup. The heat seeps into my fingers, and I take a deep breath, letting the scent of the coffee ground me in this moment.

I take a sip as I make my way to a small table by the window, my gaze drifting out toward the bustling street. The French Quarter is alive as always with musicians playing their hearts out on street corners, and the sound of a saxophone wails somewhere in the distance. It's the rhythm of my city, and I can't imagine living anywhere else.

This is my ritual: a coffee and a few minutes of stillness before heading into the bookstore. My grandmother used to say that life is made of these little moments, the quiet ones that get tucked between the bigger events. She knew what she was talking about—she'd lived a whole life within the pages of books, and I've spent my life trying to follow in her footsteps, to preserve the legacy she left me.

I glance down at the small stack of poetry books I brought with me, thumb through one of them, and smile. The day is just beginning, and I already feel at home here, in the heart of it all.

As I sit there, sipping my coffee and watching the world move outside the window, my thoughts inevitably drift to poetry. It's always been like this. Poetry finds its way into every quiet moment, every corner of my life. It's more than just words on a page; it's the language of my soul, the way I make sense of the world.

I remember the first time I fell in love with a poem. I must have been seven or eight, sitting in my grandmother's bookstore with a dusty, old copy of Walt Whitman's *Leaves of Grass* in my lap. I didn't understand half of what I was reading at the time, but there was something in Whitman's voice that stirred me and made me feel connected to something bigger than myself. "I am large, I contain multitudes," he wrote, and even as a child, that idea fascinated

The Words of Us

me—the vastness of the self, the endless possibilities within us all.

From there, I devoured every poet I could find. Emily Dickinson, with her quiet power, once wrote, "I dwell in Possibility—A fairer House than Prose." And that's what poetry became for me—a place of endless possibility, a way to step outside the ordinary and into something deeper, more profound.

When I got older, I discovered Pablo Neruda. His words had a way of lighting fires in my heart, especially his love poems. "I love you as certain dark things are to be loved, in secret, between the shadow and the soul," he wrote, and I remember feeling seen, as if he'd articulated something I hadn't yet been able to put into words. It captured the dark edges of love that was so true, and yet we seem so afraid to admit it to ourselves. Back then, loving a girl was just that: dark and secret, something that shouldn't be shared. But he made me feel like that was okay. That it was okay for me to be gay.

And then there was Audre Lorde, whose fierce voice reminded me that poetry isn't just a refuge—it's a tool, a weapon, a way to fight back against the injustices of the world. "Poetry is not a luxury. It is a vital necessity of our existence," she said, and I've carried that truth with me ever since. Poetry has saved me more times than I can count. It's the thing that makes sense when nothing else does, the place where I can be most myself.

Now, I see my bookstore as a living poem, a place where words flow from shelf to shelf, where people come to find a piece of themselves in the pages of a book. Hosting weekly open mics has become my way of sharing that love with others, of creating space for voices to be heard, for stories to be told. There's magic in watching people stand up, their heart pounding as they spill their truths, letting the words find their way home.

I smile to myself, running my fingers along the spine of a poetry book beside me, a new collection I've been waiting to dive into. Poetry is my lifeline, my compass. And no matter what happens, it's always there waiting for me in the quiet moments.

Despite my deep love for poetry, I've never been able to write it. Believe me, I've tried. There were so many nights when I sat at my desk, pen hovering over the page, waiting for the words to come. But they never did—not in the way I hoped. Every time I tried to write, it felt like I was chasing something that kept slipping through my fingers, just out of reach.

I'd start with a line, maybe two, but they never felt right. The rhythm was always off, the imagery forced. It was like my heart knew what it wanted to say, but my hand couldn't translate it. I'd crumple up page after page, feeling frustrated, like I was failing at something I was supposed to be good at. After all, I'd spent my life surrounded by books, devouring the words of the greats. Shouldn't I be able to string together something worth reading?

But eventually, I had to accept that writing wasn't my gift. Not like it was for the poets I admired. My talent wasn't in creating the words; it was in loving them, in understanding them, in helping others find the words that mattered to them. My grandmother used to tell me that not everyone is meant to write poetry; some of us are meant to carry it in our hearts, to be the keepers of it, the ones who make space for it in the world.

And so that's what I've become. A keeper of poetry. A collector of voices. I host those open mics, I fill the shelves of my bookstore with collections of verse, I listen to others pour out their hearts in a way I never could. And I'm okay with that now. It took me a long time, but I've realized that you don't have to write poetry to live it or love it.

So, while I may never pen the next great verse, I've found my place within the world of poetry. It's in the pages of the books I love, in the voices I amplify, in the quiet spaces I create for others to share their gifts. And maybe that's enough. Maybe that's more than enough.

As I leave the coffee shop, cup still warm in my hand, I step out onto the cobblestone streets of New Orleans, a city that seems to breathe with its own pulse. The morning sun filters through the canopies of live oaks draped in Spanish moss, casting dappled shadows along the sidewalks. The air is thick with humidity, but it's familiar, like an old friend I've grown used to. No longer uncomfortable, just part of the charm.

Walking through the French Quarter feels like stepping back in time, as if the history of the place rises up from the ground beneath my feet. The scent of beignets drifts on the breeze, mixing with the faint jazz notes that always seem to be playing somewhere in the background. Street performers and fortune tellers are already setting up their spots in Jackson Square, their bright clothing and tarot cards adding to the vibrant tapestry of the city. It's all part of the rhythm of New Orleans, a rhythm I've come to know well.

My bookstore sits nestled on a quieter street, a little tucked away from the constant hustle and bustle but close enough to draw in the steady stream of tourists who come to experience the soul of this city. The storefront is painted a deep, weathered green, with tall windows that showcase carefully arranged books and small trinkets from the city's culture and history. Above the door hangs the wooden sign my grandmother carved years ago—*Rousseau's Books*—marking the spot like a promise.

It's a small shop, but it does well, thriving off the mix of regulars and tourists who pass through. The locals are my bread and butter, the ones who know me by name, who stop in for their favorite poetry collections or to chat about the latest literary event in town. They're loyal, and over the years, we've built a community around this little place, bound by our love for books and words.

Then there are the tourists who flood the streets during festival season or just come to soak in the city's mystique. They're drawn to the shop for different reasons, their eyes lighting up at the sight of shelves lined with books on voodoo, the history of jazz, and, of course, New Orleans' famous connection to witches. I stock them all—Anne Rice's The Vampire Chronicles always sell well, as do books on the city's haunted past, tales of Marie Laveau, and the legacy of voodoo priestesses. There are shelves filled with guides to the cemeteries, stories of haunted mansions, and works that explore the rich Creole history that makes this place so unique. It's not exactly my passion—witchcraft and vampires—but it pays the bills. And honestly, it's fascinating in its own right, even if I'm more drawn to the quiet introspection of a poem than the dark allure of a ghost story.

Sometimes I stand behind the counter, watching the tourists browse the shelves with wide-eyed curiosity, their fascination with the macabre almost tangible. They ask for recommendations, and I steer them toward the local legends, the tales of magic that run through the veins of this city. I get it—New Orleans has that effect on people. There's a certain enchantment here, a kind of mystery that hangs in the air like the heavy fog that rolls in from the Mississippi

River at dawn. And while it's not my first love, I'm grateful for it. Because it's this interest in the city's darker side that allows my shop to thrive, that keeps the lights on and the shelves stocked.

More importantly, it's what allows me to host the open mic poetry nights, the real heart of the bookstore. Every Friday, we clear out the middle of the shop, move the tables and chairs into a makeshift audience space, and set up a small microphone by the front window. Poets from all over the city—some seasoned, some brand new—come to share their soul. The regulars, the ones who live for poetry like I do, know it's more than just a reading. It's a ritual. A space for people to pour out their hearts, to connect with others through words that might otherwise never be spoken. It's magic of a different sort, quieter, more subtle, but no less powerful.

I think my grandmother would be proud. She always believed in the power of books to bring people together and create community, and even though the store has changed over the years, I think I'm still honoring that. She used to say that books are like doorways, each one a portal into another world, another mind. And that's what I hope my shop is—a place where people can come and find those doorways, whether they're searching for the mysteries of the past or the secrets hidden in a line of verse.

As I approach the bookstore, the familiar sight of it brings a smile to my face. The sun hits the windows just right, casting a warm glow inside. I unlock the door, stepping into the quiet, welcoming space. The smell of old paper and leather bindings greets me, mingling with the faint scent of lavender from the candle I always keep burning in the corner.

It's not just a business to me; it's home. It's where I belong, surrounded by words, stories, and the living, breathing history of this city.

2

SASHA

Five years. It feels strange to say it, even stranger to believe it. I think back to that girl in the airport, the one running on empty searching for something she couldn't name. That Sasha barely resembles the one I am now. New Orleans has a way of doing that to you—changing you, making you feel like you've always belonged here, even if you showed up with nothing but a backpack and a lot of uncertainty.

I slide my fingers along the spines of the books in front of me, dusty and forgotten, tucked away on crooked shelves in this old thrift store. It's become one of my favorite haunts. There's something magical about these places, where treasures are hidden in the most unexpected corners, waiting to be discovered.

The store smells like old leather and the faint musk of time, mixed with the sweetness of patchouli incense burning by the front counter. The owner, a guy who calls himself DJ, lounges behind the register, playing some obscure jazz record that fills the space with soulful horns and steady rhythms. The kind of music that sinks into your bones and makes you feel like you're in a film noir. The whole place has that vibe, like it exists in a time loop somewhere between past and present, suspended in a world all its own.

I've gotten to know DJ pretty well over the years. He doesn't talk much, but when he does, it's always with this slow, thoughtful cadence, like every word is carefully chosen. I think he gets me. We're both the kind of people who found ourselves here by accident and stayed because we had nowhere else that felt this right.

I pull a dog-eared copy of *Beloved* by Toni Morrison off the shelf and smile to myself. It's one of those books I already own, but whenever I find it in a place like this, I feel the need to rescue it. Like someone left it behind without realizing the gift they were giving up. And maybe I can help it find a new home with someone who'll appreciate its beauty.

New Orleans fits me like a glove now. I've woven myself into the fabric of this place, meeting people at poetry readings, listening and appreciating the local artists, and trying to find my voice in the hum of the city's vibrant art scene. The spoken word community here is tight-knit, a mix of old-timers who've been around since before I knew what poetry was and newcomers who bring fresh energy with them. It's one of the things I love most about this city—how the old and the new coexist, feeding off each other, creating something alive and ever-changing.

I was nervous when I first arrived and felt like an outsider, like I didn't belong in a place with so much history and character. But that changed. Slowly, without me even realizing it, New Orleans started to feel like home. It's in the rhythm of the streets, the way people greet you with a smile and a story, the way the air is thick with both humidity and magic. It's the kind of place that lets you be whoever you want to be, as long as you're true to yourself.

I tuck the book under my arm and continue browsing, my fingers trailing over old paperbacks and faded covers. I'm not looking for anything specific, just letting the energy of the place guide me. That's the beauty of these thrift stores. You never know what you'll find, but somehow, it's always exactly what you need.

It hits me sometimes, just how much has changed since that day in JFK when I made the decision to come here with no plan, no idea what I was getting myself into. I'm not running anymore. I'm rooted now in a way I never thought I could be. The city has accepted me, and I've accepted it in return. I've found my place among the ghosts and jazz musicians, the artists and poets who call this place home.

And as I stand here in this dusty thrift store filled with relics of the past, I feel a quiet sense of contentment. I've made it. Maybe not in the way I imagined, but in a way that feels right.

The past still haunts me, though. I've come a long way from that lost girl in the airport, but some things have a way of lingering, like shadows that never fully fade. They creep up on me in the quiet moments when I'm alone with my thoughts or when I'm flipping through old books in a place like this, where time feels blurred and memories stir just beneath the surface.

Sometimes I'll be standing on a street corner, listening to the distant echo of a saxophone or performing a piece at an open mic, and suddenly, there it is—something from before. A flash of a moment I'd rather forget, an echo of the pain I worked so hard to leave behind. It doesn't cripple me like it used to, but it's always there, a quiet reminder of where I've been. The heartbreak, the mistakes, the people I hurt along the way.

I try not to let it pull me under. I've learned to live with it, to acknowledge the past without letting it define me. But every now and then, I catch myself wondering if I've really escaped it at all or if I'm just better at burying it now. There are days when its weight presses on my chest, heavy and uninvited, and I have to remind myself that I'm not that person anymore.

But still, there are times when I feel it—when the city's energy quiets and it's just me and the ghosts of who I used to be.

I didn't just leave with a backpack. I left without a number, a name, an address. No ties, no way for anyone to reach me. I was dead to my past, as distant and untraceable as the ghosts that haunt this city. It wasn't just an escape; it was a burial. I had to disappear completely to find a way to survive.

At first, it felt liberating, like shedding a skin that had grown too tight. No one could find me; no one could drag me back into the mess I'd made. I could be anyone I wanted, free from the wreckage I'd left behind. But there was a cost. Severing ties so cleanly, so completely, meant I didn't just leave the pain behind—I left everything. Every last shred of who I was, every connection, every piece of my life before. It was all gone, wiped clean.

Just like the ghosts of New Orleans that roam the streets tethered to memories and places but not to people, I became untethered. I drifted through my new life, feeling the echoes of the past and never able to go back.

∽

With my new books, I head back to my apartment in the Tremé, one of the oldest neighborhoods in New Orleans. It's not fancy, not by a long shot. The streets here are cracked and uneven, the houses a little more worn down than in the touristy parts of town. There's a mix of rusting metal fences, overgrown gardens, and brightly painted shutters that have seen better days. But it's real, authentic in a way that makes you feel connected to something deeper. This neighborhood has soul. Jazz drifts through the air at all hours, blending with the scent of fried food and the occasional bursts of laughter from a front porch gathering.

My building's nothing special—peeling paint, a stairwell that creaks with every step, and windows that rattle when the wind picks up—but it's home. The people here are good. There's Miss Yvonne, who sits outside every afternoon, fanning herself with a church bulletin and offering me sweet tea and advice about life. The couple across the hall, Andre and Camille, are musicians—he plays the trumpet, she sings—and their apartment always hums with music that spills into the hallway. It's the kind of place where people know each other's names and we all look out for each other in our own quiet ways.

Inside, my place is small, barely big enough for the essentials. The walls are painted a deep, moody blue, which I chose deliberately. I wanted the space to feel like a cocoon, a place where the outside world could melt away and I could get lost in my thoughts. The furniture is mismatched, mostly secondhand pieces I'd picked up from thrift stores or the side of the road, but I've made it work. There's a threadbare couch by the window piled with colorful throw pillows and a soft blanket I found at a flea market. My bed is tucked into a corner, draped with old quilts that smell faintly of lavender from the sachets I keep in the linen drawer.

But it's the details that make it mine. The bookshelves that line one wall are crammed full of poetry collections, some of them dog-eared and marked with notes from years of reading. I've hung framed pages of my favorite poems on the walls—Audre Lorde, Mary Oliver, Langston Hughes—each one a reminder of the voices that shaped me.

The tiny desk near the window is cluttered with notebooks, scraps of paper, pens, and candles that burn down too quickly because I'm always lighting them when I write. There's a typewriter on the floor next to it, an old relic I found at a yard sale that I never actually use but keep around because it feels like it belongs here. A worn-out armchair sits in the corner, a perfect spot for reading, with a small table beside it holding a cup of half-finished coffee, a stack of half-read books, and a journal filled with scribbled lines that might one day become poems.

Fairy lights hang haphazardly along the ceiling, casting a soft glow that makes the whole space feel warm and lived-in. I've got art scattered everywhere—photographs of jazz musicians, abstract paintings I picked up from local artists, and collages I made myself out of torn-up magazines and postcards. There's no real theme to it, just pieces that speak to me in some way. It's cluttered, but it's a creative kind of clutter, the kind that makes you feel like anything is possible.

This little apartment, with its creaky floors and chipped paint, is where I come alive. It's where I write, where I reflect, where I let the ghosts of the past drift through without letting them settle. It's not perfect, but it's mine. It's a place where I can be myself—messy, complicated, always searching—and somehow, that feels just right.

Hung up by the door next to my tattered denim jacket are my work clothes—a black t-shirt with the logo of a local wing bar plastered across the front and a pair of worn-out jeans that have seen more spills than I care to remember. I only do a few shifts a week, just enough to cover rent and keep the fridge stocked with basics, but it's far from glamorous. The wing bar's not exactly a dream gig—sticky floors, loud crowds, and the smell of fried food that clings to you long after you've clocked out—but the tips are good. Really good.

It's the kind of place where regulars come in like clockwork, and if you can smile, flirt a little, and keep their drinks full, you walk out with your pockets lined. The music is always cranked up too loud, and by the end of a shift, my feet are screaming and my voice is hoarse from shouting over the noise. But in a city like New Orleans where rent's creeping up and the freelance poetry submissions don't exactly pay the bills, it's a job I'm grateful for. Even if it means I have to scrub the grease out of my hair every other night.

I don't hate it, though. The place has a certain charm to it, the kind that only a dive bar with sticky tables and neon signs can offer. The regulars know my name, and some of the guys in the kitchen can actually make me laugh when the night slows down. It's loud, messy, and exhausting, but it's also another piece of this life I've built here, another way I stay grounded. I figure as long as I've got a place to write, a community to be a part of, and enough cash to keep the lights on, I'm doing alright.

I glance at the work clothes hanging there by the door and smile to myself. It's not forever, but for now, it's enough.

In the few years I've been here, I've made a handful of friends, but none like Glass. He's not just a friend; he's the kind of person who lights up a room without even trying, a force of creativity and personality that draws people to him like moths to a flame. We met at a poetry reading in the back of some dingy bar in the Bywater, and he stood out instantly—not just because of his sharp, angular style or the way he carried himself like a work of art, but because of the way he spoke. His words were like nothing I'd ever heard before—fluid, abstract, somehow both piercing and soft.

Even now, I don't know his birth name, and I don't ask. It's part of his mystique. He's Glass, and that's all he needs to be. The way he uses his name in his poetry is incredible. He plays with the concepts of transparency, fragility, and reflection; sometimes he's clear as glass, and other times, he's sharp enough to cut. It's like his entire identity is woven into these layers of meaning, this constant dance between how the world sees him and how he sees himself.

His poems are like puzzles, shards of language that catch the light in different ways depending on how you look at them. I remember one of his pieces vividly. It was about standing in front of a mirror and realizing that glass both reveals and conceals, that you can see through it but it also reflects back everything you're hiding. It was beautiful and haunting, like most of what he writes.

We hit it off instantly, bonding over our love of words, and now we're practically inseparable. Glass has a way of showing up at the most unexpected times, pulling me out of whatever funk I'm in with some wild story or a spontaneous idea for a new piece. He pushes me creatively and personally, in ways I didn't even know I needed. We spend hours wandering the city, talking about art and life, sometimes stopping to watch a street performer or duck into a random gallery.

Glass is the kind of friend who makes you feel like you're part of something bigger than yourself, like the world is one huge, unfolding piece of art. Even in this city full of characters, he's someone who stands out, not just because of his talent but because of the way he sees the world. And somehow, he's always made space for me in that world, even when I wasn't sure I fit anywhere.

With him around, life in New Orleans is never dull, and neither is the poetry.

3

EVIE

It's a quiet Wednesday evening, the kind of night when the bookstore feels more like a sanctuary than a business. The midweek poetry nights are smaller, more intimate, just a handful of us gathered in the soft glow of the lamps scattered around the room. The hum of the city outside feels distant, muted by the thick walls and the comforting presence of books.

These Wednesday sessions aren't as busy as the weekend ones, but there's something special about them. The regulars who come midweek are the ones who have found their rhythm here. They know the space, they know each other, and they come not just to perform but to listen, to let the words sink in more deeply without the distraction of a bustling crowd. There's a peacefulness to it, a slower, quieter appreciation for the craft.

Tonight, there's a young man standing up at the microphone. He's new to the scene, just started at the state college. He's got that fresh, eager look about him. His face is still rounded with youth, and his clothes are a little too neatly pressed, like he's trying to fit in without losing himself in the process. He's clutching a notebook in both hands, the paper shaking ever so slightly, and his eyes keep darting up from the page to the few of us scattered around the room, as if he's searching for some sign of approval.

His voice is soft, almost too soft for spoken poetry, but the words—there's something special there. He writes beautifully. His lines are intricate, delicate even, like lacework carefully stitched together. There's potential in his work, something raw and promising, but I can tell he's struggling to let it breathe in front of an audience. His shyness weighs down his delivery, making him stumble over the words and hiding the beauty of the images he's crafted behind a nervous whisper.

I sit in the back, watching him carefully and listening to the quiet brilliance of his work that's just waiting to break through. But spoken poetry might not be for him—not yet, anyway. He's the kind of writer who needs time and space to grow into his voice, to let it find the strength to match the power of his pen. I can see it, even if he can't just yet.

The others in the room are kind, offering encouraging nods and soft smiles, trying to put him at ease. He finishes his poem, his voice trailing off like he's not sure if he's really done, and there's a moment of quiet before we applaud, warm and genuine. He looks relieved, but still unsure, like he's not quite convinced he belongs here.

Afterward, he quietly retreats to a chair in the corner, his notebook clutched tightly against his chest, and I find myself hoping he'll keep coming back. He's got something, that much is clear. And maybe with time, he'll learn to let his words take up the space they deserve. For now, though, I'm just happy to have him here, to be part of his journey, even if it's only a small part.

This is why I love these midweek nights. They're quieter,

sure, but there's something about the space we create here, something that allows for growth and discovery in ways the busier weekend crowds don't always allow. It's a place for the tentative, the uncertain, the ones still finding their voice. And tonight, it feels like we've planted a seed that, with a little patience, might just bloom into something beautiful.

The door swings open, and a gust of the outside world rushes in with it—humid, heavy, and full of life. It disrupts the stillness of the bookstore, the scent of rain and street vendors mixing with the soft light inside. I glance up, half-expecting another regular, but what I see catches me entirely off guard.

She's late, bustling in with a kind of hurried energy, her presence instantly commanding the room. She has dark, windswept hair that's half pulled back, messy in the way that suggests it wasn't styled to be perfect, but it somehow works. She's breathing a little too fast, her chest rising and falling under a loose, cropped sweater, as if she'd been running to get here. Her eyes, sharp and alive, dart around the room, scanning to see if she's missed everything. They're the kind of eyes that don't just see, they *search*—deep, piercing, as if they could unravel a person with a single glance.

The moment our eyes meet, it's like the air in the room shifts. Something inside me jolts, like a spark igniting from deep within. It's intense, unexpected, and I have to remind myself to breathe. I'm rooted to the spot, my fingers curling tighter around the coffee cup in front of me, grounding myself against the sudden rush of emotion. There's a gravity to her, a force that seems to pull everything in the room toward her, even me.

She's dressed casually, but there's something about her presence that makes it feel deliberate. A pair of worn jeans, boots that look like they've seen more than a few cities, and that sweater—half falling off one shoulder, exposing a tattoo I can't quite make out from where I'm sitting. There's a quiet defiance in the way she carries herself, a sense that she's completely herself and yet somehow unpredictable.

She pauses, her eyes locking onto mine for the briefest of moments, and the intensity doubles. It's like the room narrows, the sound of shuffling papers and soft murmurs fading into the background. My heart skips—literally misses a beat—and I can't explain why. It's as if she brings the storm inside with her, carrying the weight of something more than just herself.

She exhales, and in that moment, I feel it—a connection, a pull I can't name but can't ignore. I have no idea who she is, but I know this much: I need to find out.

Just as I'm trying to get a grip on this sudden, inexplicable feeling, she stops and turns back toward the door. That's when I see him. She reaches for his hand and pulls him inside with her, like she's anchoring him to her world. They're an unlikely pair at first glance, but the way she grips his hand so naturally makes me think they must be a couple.

He is striking in a different way. Tall and lean, with a kind of ethereal presence that feels both here and not here at the same time. His skin is pale, his features sharp and angular, almost delicate, with high cheekbones that make him look like he's stepped out of a painting. His hair is cut short on the sides but long on top, a wave of platinum blond that contrasts against the dark, loose clothing he wears—an oversized black shirt and fitted jeans. His eyes are a piercing blue, sharp and clear like glass, and they seem to reflect everything around him with an intensity that mirrors hers.

Together, they create this magnetic contrast—her with her wild, restless energy and him with his quiet, almost ghostly calm. He doesn't speak, just glances around the room, taking everything in with a gaze that feels far older than his years. When their hands are clasped together, it's impossible not to notice the way they fit—two pieces of some larger puzzle, like they were made to balance each other.

I can't help but assume they're together. There's a certain ease in the way they stand next to each other, a natural closeness that suggests something deeper than friendship. For a moment, I feel a flicker of disappointment that I quickly try to shake off. It's silly, irrational even, to feel anything at all about someone I've never met before, but that pull between me and the girl from moments ago still lingers in the air like an unfinished conversation.

He steps forward, still holding her hand, and looks around the room before speaking. His voice is soft, almost too soft for a place like this, but it carries in the silence.

"Is there space for another poet tonight?" he asks, his words directed more to the room than to anyone in particular. But in a space like this, all eyes naturally turn to me.

There's a brief pause, the air hanging thick with anticipation, and I find myself nodding before I can even think about it. "Of course," I say, my voice a little steadier than I feel inside. I glance at the makeshift stage at the front of the room and back at him, catching a faint, almost imperceptible smile on his face.

The room shifts ever so slightly, the energy changing as he steps forward, and I know tonight is going to be different.

He releases her hand and steps up to the microphone, and the room seems to contract around him. His presence, understated as it is, pulls us all in. There's a kind of quiet intensity to him—nothing exaggerated, nothing forced, but something about the way he carries himself demands attention. The usual rustling of papers, shifting in seats, even the occasional cough—all of it fades away. You could hear a pin drop.

He stands there for a moment, letting the silence settle, before he begins. His voice, soft and measured, flows through the room, each word like a delicate thread connecting us all.

"We build ourselves in the reflection of another,
Construct our edges with the way they look at us,
Like glass blown in the heat of affection,
Curved and fragile, held together by the warmth of their gaze.
I stand in front of you,
A reflection of the love you've given me,
Clear, but not unbreakable—
And you don't know it, but you hold me in your hands,
Gentle at first, as if you know I'm brittle.
But then comes the pressure,
The weight of your fingers tracing lines across my surface,
And suddenly, the cracks begin to form,
Hairline fractures that start small,
Invisible unless you're looking closely.
Do you see it? Do you notice?
The way I start to chip, to splinter under your touch,
The way the light no longer bends through me the same way,
Because I am no longer whole.
And in that moment, when the glass finally shatters,
I am not the reflection you once loved,
But shards scattered at your feet,
Waiting to be swept away,
Or perhaps, pieced back together
Though I'll never be the same."

He finishes, and for a moment, no one moves. No one breathes. The words linger in the air, suspended like fragile glass themselves, shimmering with the weight of everything he just said. The room is still, the energy palpable, and it's as if we're all afraid that even the slightest sound will break the spell.

I am completely captivated. It's not just the words— though they are beautifully, hauntingly true— but it's the way he delivers them, like each line is being carefully placed into the air, delicate and intentional. He speaks of fragility, of being shattered by love, and there's something almost painfully honest in his voice, as if he knows these cracks all too well.

The room stays silent for a beat longer, and then the applause starts, soft at first then growing louder. But even as we clap, I can feel the room's hesitance to let go of the moment, to release what we've all just experienced.

He steps back, offering a faint smile as he returns to his seat beside the beautiful dark haired woman I can't stop looking back to, the spell broken but the electricity still buzzing in the air.

4

SASHA

We'd barely made it. Glass had heard about this place through a friend of a friend, and by the time we crossed town, we were already late. Typical. I could feel the weight of my notebooks in my bag, the familiar pressure of the poems I carry with me everywhere, but tonight wasn't about me. It rarely is when Glass performs. He has this way of commanding a room that makes my own voice feel quieter in comparison—not in a bad way, but in a way that makes me step back and listen, to let him take the stage while I watch. Our styles are too different, like two sides of the same coin, and when he speaks, the air changes.

The door swings open, and I rush in, bringing the heavy night air with me. My eyes sweep across the room, hoping we haven't missed everything. I glance around quickly, scanning the small crowd—and that's when I see her.

She's sitting at the back of the room, barely lit by the soft lamps scattered around the bookstore. Her presence hits me like a punch to the chest, unexpected and intense. She's holding a coffee cup, her fingers curled around it like she's trying to steady herself. There's something about her that pulls me in instantly, as if I've known her in another life—or at least that's what it feels like. Her rich brown hair is pulled back loosely, her skin glows faintly in the dim light, and her eyes... God, her eyes. They're sharp but soft, like she's watching the world and trying to understand it all at once.

My heart skips, and for a second, all I want to do is walk straight over to her. To sit across from her, maybe not even say anything—just be in her presence and know her somehow. It's a strange feeling, sudden and insistent, like a magnet pulling me toward her. I don't even know her name, but I'm already drawn to her in a way I can't explain. The bookstore seems smaller suddenly, the rest of the room fading into the background as I imagine what it would be like to sit beside her, to feel the warmth of her gaze on me.

But then, I remember Glass.

I glance back at him still standing in the doorway behind me and pull him forward instinctively. It's not time to indulge whatever this feeling is; I have a friend to support. I weave through the chairs with him, my hand still gripping his as I pull him toward the front of the room. We sit down, side by side, and I let the tension in my body ease as I take in the cozy, intimate space.

As Glass steps up to the microphone, the room quietens, and I feel the energy shift again. He's in his element now, and I lean forward in my chair, letting the anticipation settle over me. Even though I've heard him perform countless times, every time feels like the first. His words always hit somewhere deep, in a place I sometimes forget exists until he reminds me.

When he begins, I feel the first stirrings of emotion rising in my chest. His poem cuts through me, every line about love's fragility, about the way we shatter ourselves in the hands of those we trust. And as he speaks, I can feel my heart splintering along with the images he creates. His voice, soft and steady, weaves through the room, and I can't hold back the tears.

They come slowly at first, silent and warm, trailing down my cheeks as I listen. I don't wipe them away. I let them fall because there's something cathartic about it, something cleansing in letting the emotion pass through me. Glass speaks of fragility, but what he doesn't say is that in breaking, we can also find a kind of beauty. A kind of strength in knowing that we were once whole, even if we aren't now.

When he finishes, the room is still for a beat longer, and I blink away the remaining tears, trying to collect myself. I glance back, almost instinctively, to see if she's still there—the woman at the back. And she is still watching us with that same intense gaze. The pull is still there, stronger now.

But for now, I stay where I am.

Glass finishes his performance, and for a moment, the room lingers in that silence that always follows something powerful. But then, like clockwork, people start to stand, the gentle murmur of conversation filling the space again. The regulars know the drill—chairs get stacked, tables moved back to their places. There's a kind of rhythm to it, and without needing much direction, Glass and I follow their lead, adding our chairs to the growing pile in the corner.

A few people approach Glass, eager to introduce themselves. They're kind, warm, and clearly taken with his performance. One of the older women—a regular by the looks of it—clutches a small stack of books to her chest as she asks, "You coming back, honey? You should. Your work...well, it moved me. We get a bigger crowd on the weekends, though, so you'd really kill it then."

He smiles politely, dipping his head slightly. "Thank

you. I'd love to come back, but I can't make weekends too often. I work a lot of late shifts, but Wednesdays"—he glances over at me for confirmation, and I smile back—"I think Wednesdays might be my new thing."

There's a shared sense of approval in the room, and people nod in understanding. But her words stick with me: The weekends are better, bigger crowds. As Glass continues his polite conversations, promising to return, I find myself turning the idea over in my mind. I've been coming to poetry events with Glass, always content to let him take the stage, but something about the energy here tonight, the quiet yet engaged crowd, makes me think that maybe I could step up next time. Maybe the bigger crowd on Friday would be the push I need to finally read something of my own.

The thought simmers in the back of my mind as we finish tidying up and say our goodbyes. I tell myself that I might just come back on Friday, notebook in hand. Maybe it's time to stop hiding behind Glass's performances and let my own voice be heard.

As I gather my bag and notebook, the thought of Friday still lingering, I can't help but think about the woman. The one who seemed to pull me in the moment I walked through the door. I scan the room, hoping to catch another glimpse of her, but she's nowhere to be seen. Did she leave already? Did I miss my chance to...what? Say hello? Ask her name? I'm not even sure what I was hoping for, but the tug of disappointment settles in my chest.

Just as I turn to leave, I see her. She's behind the counter now, quietly stacking books with an easy grace, her hair slightly tousled from the evening. She's focused, but there's a softness to her movements, like this is where she belongs, tending to her little corner of the world in the quiet moments of the night.

For a split second, our eyes meet again, and my heart skips a beat just like before. The intensity from earlier returns, a steady hum in the background that I can't quite shake. She doesn't say anything—just offers a small, polite smile as she continues with her work.

And I realize that maybe coming back on Friday isn't just about the poetry after all.

∼

Thursday rolls around, and I find myself in one of New Orleans' many parks, sprawled out on a bench under the shade of a large oak tree. The sun is high, but the heat isn't unbearable yet. The air is thick with the familiar southern humidity, but there's a light breeze today, one that carries the faint scent of magnolias and damp earth. It's the kind of weather that feels heavy on your skin but comforting at the same time, like being wrapped in a warm blanket you can't quite escape.

The park is alive with the usual characters. A group of kids races past on bicycles, their laughter cutting through the quiet. Nearby, an older man sits on a bench with a newspaper folded on his lap, nodding along to the sound of a saxophone playing in the distance. The music floats through the trees, slow and melancholic, as if the city itself is taking a deep breath between the busy hours of the morning and the chaos that will inevitably arrive in the evening.

Across the lawn, there's a woman walking her dog—an enormous mutt with a shaggy coat and a smile that seems too big for its face. They move slowly, meandering through the park like they have nowhere to be, and I find myself watching them for a moment, feeling a pang of something that's both loneliness and comfort. New Orleans is full of people like this—people who take their time, who move at their own pace, who seem to understand that life here isn't about the destination but the moments you live along the way.

I've got my notebook open on my lap and a half-empty iced coffee sitting on the bench beside me. The pages are scattered with thoughts from last night—scribbles and phrases that don't quite form a complete picture yet but are circling around something I know is there, just waiting to come together. The bookstore, Glass's performance, that woman behind the counter—all of it lingers in my mind, and I can't shake the need to write it out and make sense of it.

The words come slowly at first, like they're testing the waters. I write about fragility, about the way we create ourselves in the image of others, and how easily that image can shatter. But there's something else in there, something more hopeful. Last night felt like the beginning of something—not just for Glass, but for me. It's as if the city itself, with all its ghosts and history, is offering me a space to finally say the things I've been holding back.

A warm gust of wind blows through the trees, rustling the leaves and carrying with it the distant chatter of a group of people playing frisbee nearby. The park is full of life and of stories, and I find myself drawing energy from it. There's a rhythm to New Orleans that gets into your bones if you let it, a pulse that makes everything seem more alive, more real. The city is always creating, always renewing itself, and I feel that same pull within me.

I write about the connection I felt last night, about the woman whose eyes seemed to see right through me in that split second before I pulled Glass toward the front of the room. There was something there, something I can't explain, but I'm letting the feeling guide me now, letting it pour into the poem I'm shaping. It's not perfect yet—far from it—but the ideas are there, raw and honest, just waiting to be refined.

I sit back for a moment, closing my eyes and letting the sounds of the park wash over me: the soft clink as a couple nearby sets up a picnic, the steady buzz of cicadas in the distance, the low rumble of a streetcar somewhere on the other side of the trees. I breathe it all in, the essence of this city that I've come to love so much.

The sun begins to sink lower in the sky, casting long shadows across the grass, but I'm in no hurry to leave. I can feel the energy of the day seeping into my work, pushing me forward. Friday is coming fast, and for the first time in a long while, I'm ready to step up and speak, to take the stage and let my voice be heard.

Inspired by the quiet magic of the park, the people moving through it like characters in their own stories, and the lingering emotion of last night, I start to write again—this time with more certainty. There's something here, something worth sharing, and I'm determined to see it through.

I glance down at my phone, and the peaceful rhythm I'd settled into suddenly shatters. The time blinks back at me. Damn, I'm running late. My shift at the wing place starts in less than an hour, and I'm all the way across town.

I quickly cap my pen and shove my notebook into my bag, my mind already switching gears. As much as I'd love to stay here lost in the words, reality calls. The wing place isn't exactly a dream job, but I need every last dollar if I want to keep this city as my home.

With one last look at the park, I sling my bag over my shoulder and start heading toward the street, the echoes of the day's writing still lingering in my mind. There's always something about New Orleans, something that keeps me going, even on the busiest days.

I weave through the usual midday crowds, stepping back into the rhythm of the city.

~

It's the end of the night, and the restaurant is finally winding down. The last group of regulars has finished up their wings and beers, and I've already started clearing the tables, wiping down surfaces, and stacking menus for the next shift. The usual chatter has died down, leaving the faint hum of the kitchen and the soft clink of glassware as Jackson and the rest of the crew wrap up. I'm tired, but it's the kind of tired that feels good. The shift went smoothly, and the tips were better than usual.

I slip behind the counter, untying my apron and folding it neatly before hanging it up. "Goodnight, Jackson," I call out, flashing him a grin as I stretch my arms, feeling the tension ease out of my back.

Jackson is behind the bar, wiping it down with a rag, his usual laid-back smirk plastered across his face. He's been running this place for years, and he's got that cool, unbothered attitude that comes from seeing it all. He looks up at me and waves me over.

"Hold on a sec, Sasha." He pulls a thick wad of cash out of the register and flips through the bills. He counts out my tips, dropping them into a small envelope before handing it over. "This is for you. You did good tonight. Tables were happy, beers were flowing, and the regulars wouldn't shut up about your smile." He winks as he hands me the envelope.

I take it from him, surprised by the weight of it. "Wow, this feels like a lot," I say, thumbing through the bills. It's more than I expected, a decent haul for a weekday shift.

Jackson grins. "Like I said, you've got a way with the regulars. They like you, Sasha. You keep 'em happy, and they keep coming back."

I shake my head with a smile, tucking the envelope into my bag. "Well, it's nice to be appreciated. But I think I'm off tomorrow," I say, leaning against the counter, "so don't expect any more magic until Saturday night."

"Right, right," Jackson says, snapping his fingers. "You've got the weekend shift. That's gonna be another busy one, so rest up."

I'm about to head for the door when Jackson chuckles, glancing over at me with that teasing glint in his eye. "You know," he says, "if those regulars knew you're gay, you probably wouldn't be pulling half the tips you do."

I can't help but roll my eyes at his remark, but I play along, leaning back against the counter with a grin. "Please," I say, my voice dripping with sarcasm, "if they knew, it would probably just add to their fantasies."

Jackson lets out a loud, genuine laugh, shaking his head as he finishes wiping down the bar. "Yeah, you're probably right about that," he says, still chuckling. "Hell, some of 'em might tip you even more."

I laugh, too, the banter easy between us. We've had this exchange before, and there's something lighthearted and fun about it. Jackson's never weird about it, just enjoys poking fun where he can, and I know it's all in good humor.

I sling my bag over my shoulder, feeling the weight of the tips resting inside. It's more than enough to get me through the week, and knowing I've got Saturday night to look forward to feels like a good balance. There's something grounding about this routine—working hard, making good money, and still having enough left in me to chase after the things that really matter: poetry, writing, and maybe, just maybe, the chance to stand in front of a crowd and let them hear my voice for once.

As I push open the door and step out into the warm New Orleans night, I take a deep breath, feeling the energy of the city wash over me. The air is thick with humidity, but it's comforting, familiar. It wraps around me like the constant hum of the streets—alive, always moving, just like I am.

5

EVIE

The bookstore is quiet today, quieter than usual for a Thursday afternoon. The occasional creak of the floorboards beneath my feet and the soft rustle of pages being turned by a single customer are the only sounds filling the space. I should feel content—the place is running smoothly, the shelves are neatly arranged, and there's a calmness in the air that would have normally soothed me. But today, the stillness feels heavy, like a weight pressing down on my chest.

I take a deep breath, settling into the worn leather chair behind the counter, and allow myself a moment of reflection. It's been years since I'd inherited this bookstore from my grandmother, and in many ways, it's become my whole world. I've poured my heart into every inch of this place: curating the shelves with care, hosting poetry readings, and fostering a community that feels like home. On the surface, everything is going well. The regulars keep coming back, and the steady influx of tourists ensures that business is never too slow. By most standards, this is success.

And yet, it's not enough. Not entirely.

The problem isn't with the bookstore; it's with me. I've felt it for a while now, this creeping sense of stagnation in my personal life. I've become so consumed by the rhythms of running the store and of taking care of everyone else that I've forgotten how to take care of myself. Or maybe I've just been avoiding it. Either way, something feels missing, and I don't have to look far to know what it is—romance, companionship, connection. The things I've pushed aside ever since the last heartbreak left me feeling like I was standing in the wreckage of my own life, unsure of how to rebuild.

I let out a sigh, rubbing my thumb absentmindedly over the smooth surface of my coffee cup. The memory of that last relationship is still fresh, even though it's been years. Her name was Claire. She was everything I thought I wanted: a brilliant, charming, and passionate woman. But passion has a way of burning too hot sometimes, and eventually, we both got scorched by the flames. When it ended, it felt like a piece of me had been torn away, and in the aftermath, I retreated into the safety of the bookstore, throwing myself into the familiar comfort of books and the quiet routine of my days. It was easier that way, safer. I convinced myself that I didn't need love, not when I had this place. But now, I'm not so sure.

My thoughts drift back to last night's poetry reading. It had been an ordinary Wednesday—quiet, intimate, the kind of night where the regulars gathered, and the energy was low but warm. And then she walked in.

I can't get her out of my mind. She arrived late, her presence rushing in like a gust of wind, shaking the calm stillness of the bookstore. There was something electric about her, something that drew me in from the moment I saw her. Dark, restless hair framed her face, and her green eyes— they were intense, searching, like she was looking for something but wasn't sure what. For a brief moment, our eyes locked, and it was as if the air between us shifted. I felt something then, something I haven't felt in a long time—a spark, a stirring deep inside me that I didn't expect. It's been so long since I've allowed myself to feel anything like that, to even consider the possibility of letting someone in again. And yet, there she was, a stranger, pulling at something buried inside me.

I set my coffee cup down and reach for my journal, an old leather-bound notebook I keep tucked beneath the counter. Writing has always been my way of making sense of things, of working through the thoughts and emotions that I can't quite articulate in the moment. I open it to a blank page and stare at it for a moment, the pen hovering just above the paper as I search for the words.

What am I afraid of? I begin, the words coming slowly at first. *It's been years since Claire left, and I've been fine. Fine in the sense that I've learned how to be alone, how to build a life that's full without the need for someone else to fill it. But lately, I'm not sure that's enough. Last night, when I saw her—the woman who walked in late, the one with that wild energy—I felt something. It was brief, a flicker, but it was there. A reminder that maybe, just maybe, I still have the capacity to feel something for someone. And that terrifies me.*

I pause, my pen hovering as I think back to that moment. What was it about her that struck me so deeply? Was it the way she seemed so alive, so full of energy and possibility? Or was it something more—a recognition of something I've been missing in myself for far too long?

Maybe it's easier to stay closed off, I write. *Maybe it's easier to hide behind the routine of the bookstore, to focus on the things I can control. But that's not living, is it? That's just surviving. And I want more than that, don't I?*

I sit back in my chair, the weight of the words sinking in. I do want more. I've always wanted more. I just haven't allowed myself to acknowledge it because doing so would mean confronting the fear that has kept me walled off for so long. The fear of getting hurt again, of opening myself up to someone only to be left standing in the wreckage once more.

But last night felt like a crack in that wall—a small crack, but a crack nonetheless. And now I'm left wondering if it's worth exploring. If it's worth seeing what's on the other side of that fear. Maybe that's what life is about, after all—taking the risks, even when you're scared. Especially when you're scared.

I close the journal and run my fingers along the worn edges of the leather cover. There's something comforting about the familiar texture beneath my fingertips, but there's also something unsettling about the realization that's beginning to form in my mind. If I'm being honest with myself, I've been hiding behind this bookstore for far too long. I've allowed it to become my whole world because it's safe. But safety isn't the same as fulfillment, and I think I've been confusing the two.

I stand up, stretching out my legs as I glance around the empty store. The shelves are lined with stories—stories of love, loss, adventure, and discovery. Stories that I've surrounded myself with for years, but never fully allowed myself to live. Maybe it's time for that to change.

The bell above the door jingles softly, and I glance up to see a customer entering. It's one of the regulars, a kind older man who comes in every Thursday to browse the poetry section. I offer him a smile and nod in acknowledgment before turning my attention back to the store.

As I walk through the aisles, straightening books and

tidying up, my thoughts keep returning to that woman. I don't even know her name, but she's left an impression on me, one that I can't seem to shake. I wonder if she felt it too—the connection, the spark—or was it just me being caught off guard by something I didn't expect to feel again?

Either way, it doesn't change the fact that something inside me has shifted. And now I'm left with the question: Am I ready? Ready to open myself up again, to take the risk of letting someone in, even if it means facing the possibility of heartbreak?

I don't know the answer yet. But what I do know is that I'm tired of living my life on the sidelines, of watching others experience the kind of connection I've been avoiding for so long. Maybe it's time to take a step forward, to allow myself to be vulnerable again. Even if it scares me.

With that thought in mind, I head back to the counter and pick up my journal once more. Flipping to a new page, I begin to write again, this time with more certainty.

Sometimes, the only way to move forward is to break through the walls you've built around yourself. To take a chance on something new, even when you're not sure where it will lead. Because maybe, just maybe, what's waiting on the other side is exactly what you've been searching for all along.

I close the journal and place it back under the counter, feeling a sense of resolve settle over me. The bookstore may be my sanctuary, but it doesn't have to be my prison. There's a whole world out there waiting to be explored—people, places, experiences I've yet to discover. And maybe, just maybe, she's part of that world.

As the day winds down and the sun begins to set outside the windows, I find myself feeling something I haven't felt in a long time: hope. Hope that, perhaps, I'm ready to take the first step toward something new. And that's enough for now.

Friday arrives with its usual buzz, the city's energy humming at a higher frequency as the weekend begins to unfold. In the French Quarter, people are already spilling into the streets, filling cafes and bars, their laughter mixing with the distant echo of jazz that seems to be ever-present in the background. But inside the bookstore, everything is still—for now.

The morning light filters through the tall windows, casting soft golden rays across the rows of bookshelves. I've been up since dawn, fussing over every small detail, making sure everything is in its place for tonight's poetry event. It's going to be a big one; I can feel it. The weekends always draw a larger crowd, a mix of familiar faces and curious newcomers. But tonight feels different. There's an anticipation hanging in the air, a subtle tension that's been building inside me since Wednesday night.

I wipe down the counter for what must be the third time, trying to channel my nervous energy into something productive. My thoughts keep drifting back to her. That woman who walked into the bookstore on Wednesday night like a gust of wind, all wild energy and intensity. I haven't been able to stop thinking about her since, and it's left me in a state of restless anticipation. I keep wondering if she'll come back tonight, if she'll stand in the same room as me again and what that might mean. It's strange to feel this way —nervous and excited all at once—but the feeling is there, unmistakable.

I've always been good at managing events like this. The bookstore may be quiet most days, but on nights like these, it comes alive in a way that reminds me why I do this. Poetry nights are my favorite. There's something magical about watching people step up to the microphone and spill their hearts out, raw and vulnerable. I love the way the words fill the room, lingering in the air like incense, transforming the space into something sacred.

But tonight, as I prepare for the event, I find myself more distracted than usual. The memory of her intense gaze lingers in my mind, and I can't help but wonder what it would be like to talk to her. To really talk to her, not just exchange glances from across the room. There was something about her—something I can't quite put my finger on—that made me feel alive in a way I haven't felt in years. It's a feeling I've been trying to ignore and push down, but it keeps bubbling up, no matter how hard I try to focus on my work.

The hours seem to drag as the day stretches on. I busy myself with setting up the chairs, making sure there's enough space for the crowd I'm expecting. I pull out the microphone and sound system, testing it just to be sure everything's in working order. My hands move through the motions, but my mind is elsewhere, drifting between thoughts of tonight and the possibilities it holds.

By late afternoon, the bookstore is ready. The chairs are neatly arranged in rows, the microphone stands tall at the front, and the small stage is set. The only thing missing is the crowd. I take a deep breath, trying to steady myself, but the nervous excitement inside me only grows. I find myself glancing at the door every few minutes, half-expecting her to walk in early. But the door remains closed, and the bookstore stays quiet.

I retreat to the back of the store where my small office is tucked away behind the stacks of books. I sit at my desk, staring at my journal, willing myself to write something that will ease the tension swirling in my chest. But the words don't come easily today. Instead, I find myself doodling absentmindedly in the margins, spirals and shapes that reflect the restlessness inside me.

What if she doesn't come? The thought crosses my mind unbidden, and I try to brush it off. It shouldn't matter if she comes or not. The poetry night will go on, the crowd will gather, and the words will flow just as they always do. But deep down, I know it does matter. Her presence changed something in me, stirred something that I thought had long since settled into quiet. If she comes back tonight, what then? Do I let myself feel whatever this is, or do I retreat into the safety of the routine I've built for myself?

The thought of facing her again, of looking into those intense green eyes, both excites and terrifies me. It's been so long since I've allowed myself to feel anything like this, so long since I've even considered the possibility of letting someone in again. But there's no denying the pull, the connection that I felt the moment our eyes met. And now, I'm left wondering if it's worth the risk to explore it further.

As the sun begins to set, casting long shadows across the floor, I step out of my office and back into the bookstore. The golden light has shifted to a soft twilight, and I can feel the city outside coming alive in a way only New Orleans can. The first few customers trickle in, regulars who always arrive early to claim their favorite seats. I greet them with a smile, exchanging the usual pleasantries, but my mind is still elsewhere, still waiting for the moment when the door swings open and she walks in.

The clock ticks closer to the event's start time, and more

people begin to arrive. The bookstore starts to fill with the familiar buzz of voices, the low murmur of conversation as people find their seats and settle in. I move through the crowd, offering smiles and adjusting chairs, but all the while, my eyes keep drifting to the door.

And then, just as the event is about to begin, the door opens.

I turn, my heart skipping a beat, and there she is. She's dressed casually again—jeans, a loose sweater, her dark hair pulled back in a way that looks effortless but beautiful. Her eyes scan the room, and for a brief moment, I think she might be looking for me. My breath catches in my throat, and I force myself to smile and stay calm, even as the nervous excitement inside me flares up all over again.

This time she is alone. Maybe she isn't with that guy after all.

She spots an empty seat near the front and makes her way toward it, her movements full of that same restless energy I noticed the first time I saw her. She sits down, glancing around as if taking in the space, and I can't help but wonder what she's thinking. Does she remember me? Did she feel the same connection that I did?

The crowd continues to settle in, and soon the room is packed. The buzz of conversation dies down as the first poet steps up to the microphone, and the event begins. I take my usual place at the back of the room, watching the poets speak, their words filling the space with emotion and meaning. But tonight, I'm more distracted than usual. My gaze keeps drifting toward her, watching the way she listens intently, her body language shifting ever so slightly with each new poem.

And I can't help but feel that tonight is different—that something is building between us, even if it's unspoken, even if it's only in the way we keep catching each other's glances from across the room. It's a quiet tension, one that simmers just beneath the surface, waiting for the right moment to boil over.

As the evening progresses, I find myself wondering what will happen when the event ends. Will she leave without a word, slipping back into the night as easily as she entered? Or will she stay, linger for a moment, and give me the chance to finally talk to her? I don't know the answer, but the anticipation of it keeps me on edge, the nervous excitement growing stronger with every passing minute.

And so, as the last poet steps up to the microphone, I prepare myself for whatever comes next. The calm before the crowd has passed, and now, the tension is reaching its peak. She is here, and I have no idea what that means for the rest of the night—or for the rest of my carefully constructed world. But for the first time in a long while, I'm ready to find out.

6

SASHA

I knew I was coming back tonight. The moment I left on Wednesday, I knew. The pull is undeniable. It isn't just about the poetry or the cozy warmth of the bookstore that has already started to feel familiar. There is something deeper, something that has been building since I first stepped foot in this place. Part of me wants to chalk it up to the energy of the city—the way New Orleans has a habit of weaving itself into your skin and pulling you into its rhythm. But I know it's more than that.

It is her.

I haven't been able to get her out of my mind since Wednesday. I try to convince myself otherwise, try to pretend that the draw I feel is nothing more than a fleeting curiosity. But that isn't true. It isn't just curiosity; it is something more intense, something electric that sparks the moment I see her behind the counter, and it lingers in the back of my mind like a melody I can't shake.

I don't know what to make of it, don't even know what I want from it. I came to New Orleans to find something new, to rewrite my story, but I hadn't been looking for this. I hadn't been looking for her. Still, that doesn't change the fact that the pull is there, undeniable and insistent, tugging at me with each passing thought. Maybe that's why I'm so nervous tonight—because I know that if I step up to that microphone, if I bare my soul in front of this crowd, she will be there, watching, listening, seeing a piece of me I haven't shared with anyone in a long time.

That scares me. But it also excites me.

When I arrive, the bookstore is already filling up, the low hum of conversation bouncing off the walls.

It is the same as before yet different. The energy is more intense tonight, buzzing with anticipation as people find their seats and prepare for the night ahead. I take a spot near the front, sliding into a chair with my notebook held close to my chest. My heart is already racing, but it isn't just because of the crowd. It's because of her.

I glance around, scanning the room, and there she is— the owner, standing near the back, her eyes moving over the crowd like she was taking everything in. I watch her for a moment, trying to steady the fluttering in my chest. She looks different tonight, more relaxed maybe, but there is still that quiet intensity about her. She moves through the space like she belongs there, like she is an extension of the bookstore itself—rooted, solid, but with a warmth that makes you want to get closer.

Her gaze shifts, and for a split second, our eyes meet. My breath catches in my throat, and I quickly look away, pretending to focus on my notebook. But the connection is there, even if it is brief. It feels like a jolt, like electricity sparking between us across the room. I'm not sure if she feels it, too, or if I'm just imagining things, but the weight of that moment stays with me, lingering in the space between us.

The Words of Us

I had told myself that I was here tonight for the poetry, that this was just another chance to immerse myself in the words and energy of the event. But deep down, I knew that wasn't the full truth. I am here because of her. I wanted to see her again, to feel that connection again, to find out if it is something real or just a figment of my imagination.

As the poets begin to read, I try to focus, to let their words wash over me, but I can't stop thinking about her. I keep stealing glances in her direction, watching the way she moves, the way her eyes follow the poets on stage, the way she smiles softly at the ones she knows. There is something magnetic about her, something that draws me in even when I try to resist it. And maybe that is part of the problem—I don't want to resist it.

I've been running for so long—running from my past, from my mistakes, from the vulnerability that comes with opening myself up to someone new. I have built my walls carefully, methodically, keeping people at a distance so that I don't get hurt again. But now, sitting here in this bookstore, I can feel those walls starting to crack. It isn't just the poetry; it's her. She is the one chipping away at my defenses, and the scariest part is that I'm not sure I want her to stop.

I don't know much about her. I don't know what her story is, what her past holds, or what she wants out of life. But that doesn't seem to matter. What matters is that every time our eyes meet, every time she smiles in my direction, I feel a spark of something new, something I haven't felt in a long time.

And it terrifies me.

But it also makes me feel alive in a way I haven't felt in years.

The night wears on, and with each passing poem, I can feel the tension inside me building. My notebook sits unopened in my lap, my fingers tracing the edges of the pages as I debate whether or not to read tonight. I had come here with the intention of performing, sharing the poem I had written. But now, sitting here with her just a few feet away, the idea of exposing that part of myself feels overwhelming.

Still, something keeps pushing me forward. Maybe it's the poem I have written—the one about walls and fragility, about how love can break us but also make us whole again. Maybe it's the fact that I have been hiding behind those walls for too long, and I am tired of running. Or maybe it's her, sitting there in the back of the room, watching me with those quiet, intense dark brown eyes, silently urging me to take the leap.

Whatever it is, I can't ignore it any longer.

The poet before me finishes their poems, and the emcee steps up to the microphone, ready to call the next name. My heart pounds in my chest, and I can feel the blood rushing in my ears, but I don't hesitate. I stand up before she can call a different name.

"I'd like to read something," I say, my voice stronger than I expected.

All eyes turn toward me, and for a moment, I feel the weight of the room pressing down on me. But then I glance back at her, and our eyes meet once again. This time, I don't look away. I hold her gaze, feeling that same electric pull between us. In that moment, everything else fades away—the nerves, the fear, the doubt. All that matters is the connection between us and the poem I am about to share.

She nods permission to me.

I step up to the microphone, my notebook clutched tightly in my hands. The lights are bright and the room is silent, but I feel a strange sense of calm wash over me. I had started this poem weeks ago, before I ever set foot in this bookstore. But now, as I stand there, ready to read it aloud, it feels like these words are meant for this moment.

"This poem is called 'We Build Our Walls,'" I say, my voice steady but soft. "It's about the way we protect ourselves and how love can both break us and rebuild us at the same time."

I take a deep breath and begin.
"We build our walls with fragile care,
Thin as glass, they're always there.
A single look, a fleeting glance,
Can break them down with just a chance.
I saw you once, you caught my eye,
And something in me wondered why.
A crack appeared, but not from pain—
A chance to build it all again.
We write ourselves in love's soft light,
In moments brief, yet burning bright.
And though we shatter, though we fall,
We rise again, and that's worth it all."

As I speak, the words feel different than when I had written them—fuller, more alive. I'm not just speaking them into the air; I'm speaking them into the space between me and her, letting her hear the truth of what I have been holding inside.

When I finish, the room is still for a moment, as if everyone is taking a collective breath. And then, the applause comes. Soft at first, then louder, filling the room with warmth and acceptance. I step back from the microphone, my heart still racing, but the sense of relief that washes over me is undeniable.

I glance back at her as I make my way back to my seat. She is clapping, too, her eyes meeting mine with that same quiet intensity. But there is something different now—a softness, an understanding that hasn't been there before. And in that moment, I know that coming back tonight has been the right choice. I have let the walls come down just a little, and it feels like the first step toward something new. Something that can grow into whatever comes next.

As the night continues, I feel lighter, freer. I don't know what is going to happen between me and her, whether this connection is something real or just a passing spark. But for now, that doesn't matter. What matters is that I have taken the first step. I let myself be seen, and it is enough.

The rest, whatever it is, will come when it is ready.

The crowd starts to thin out, and the energy in the bookstore has shifted to that soft hum that always comes after a night of poetry. People linger in small groups, their conversations low but buzzing with the excitement of what they'd just experienced. I'm still riding the high of having read my poem, feeling lighter, like I've left something behind on that stage.

But now, with the night winding down, my thoughts aren't on poetry anymore. They are on her. I have been stealing glances at her all evening, feeling that quiet tension that had started between us on Wednesday, and now, with the crowd thinning, it feels like there is finally space for something more to happen.

She is still behind the counter, tidying up and exchanging smiles with the regulars. I can feel my heart thumping in my chest, a nervous energy building as I wonder if I had the guts to talk to her. Part of me wants to walk out, to leave it as it is—a fleeting connection that will live in the charged air between us and never be explored. But something else, something stronger, pulls me toward her.

I don't overthink it. Before I know what I'm doing, I walk up to the counter, my feet moving before my mind can catch up. I feel that familiar flutter in my stomach as I get closer, but I push through it.

When she looks up and sees me standing there, her eyes brighten. I can see the recognition, that same intensity flickering in her gaze, and for a moment, it feels like the whole room has disappeared, like it is just the two of us.

"Hey," I say, my voice a little quieter than I intended. "I just wanted to say thank you. For the space, I mean. For the chance to read. It meant a lot."

Her smile widens, and it's warm, genuine. "I'm glad you did. Your poem, it was beautiful. It really resonated with me."

I feel a rush of heat rise to my cheeks. Compliments on my poetry always hit me differently than anything else; they felt personal, like someone was seeing a part of me I didn't often reveal. But coming from her, it feels even more intense.

"Thank you," I reply, not quite sure what else to say, but not wanting the conversation to end. "I've been writing for a while, but it's rare that I get the chance—well, the courage—to share. This place feels special."

She nods, her eyes softening. "That's what I hope for. My grandmother always believed that words had the power to connect people, to heal, even. I've tried to keep that spirit alive here. I am Evie. Evie Rousseau."

I lean against the counter, feeling the conversation start to flow more easily. "Sasha Bennett." I offer my name, gifting it to her, as she did to me. "It definitely feels like that. This city has a way of drawing people in, doesn't it? Like it's full of ghosts and stories that are just waiting to be heard."

She smiles again, this time with a hint of amusement in her eyes. "Yeah, something like that."

The conversation keeps going, and we talk about poetry, about the bookstore, about writing and words. We're chatting like old friends, the back-and-forth coming so naturally, that I barely notice the time passing. Every now and then, someone approaches the counter, looking for help or to make a purchase, but Evie barely notices. She glances over at them and offers a quick smile, but her attention keeps returning to me, her eyes locked on mine as we talk about everything and nothing all at once.

At one point, I hear a soft cough, followed by a subtle throat clearing. It snaps us both out of our conversation, and I turn to see a small line of people waiting at the counter, looking a little impatient.

"Oh." Evie's eyes widen as she realizes how long we've been talking. "I'm so sorry," she says quickly to the customers, her cheeks flushing a deep shade of red as she steps away to help them.

I can feel my own face heating up, a mix of embarrassment and amusement washing over me. We have been so engrossed in each other that we haven't even noticed the world moving on around us.

I linger near the counter for a moment, waiting for her to finish with the customers, trying to decide if I should leave now or stick around. Part of me doesn't want the night to end, doesn't want to walk away from whatever this is that has started between us.

When she finishes helping the last person, Evie turns back to me, still looking a little flustered but smiling. "Sorry about that," she says, laughing softly. "I guess we got a little carried away."

"No need to apologize," I say, smiling back. "It was nice talking with you. Really nice."

There's a beat of silence, a pause in the air between us, and I can feel the question forming in my mind before I even realize what I am going to say.

"Would you..." I hesitate, suddenly nervous again, but I push through it. "Would you like to continue this conversation? Maybe over coffee tomorrow?"

Evie's smile softens, and for a second, I think I see something flicker in her eyes—something that makes my heart skip a beat.

"I'd like that," she says, her voice soft but certain. "There's a cafe just around the corner. How about noon?"

"Noon sounds perfect," I reply, feeling that flutter in my chest again, but this time it's mixed with excitement.

We exchange a few more words—small details about where to meet—and then, with one last smile, I make my way to the door. As I step out into the warm night air, I felt lighter, like something inside me has shifted, cracked open in a way that I wasn't expecting.

7

EVIE

The night is quiet, but my mind won't stop racing. I'm lying in bed, staring at the ceiling, but all I can think about is her—Sasha. The conversation we had after the poetry event plays over and over in my head like a song stuck on repeat. The way she smiled when she talked about writing, how her eyes sparkled when she mentioned New Orleans, the way her voice dipped slightly when she said my name for the first time. It's all there, vivid and insistent, tugging at me in the stillness of my bedroom.

Usually, after these poetry nights, there's a sense of closure. The words have been spoken, the poets have left, and the air in the bookstore is heavy with a kind of lingering calm. Spoken poetry has always had a special appeal to me because of its transience. It's fleeting, something that happens in a moment and then vanishes, like smoke dissipating into the night. You can't keep it. You can't hold it. You can only experience it as it happens and then let it go.

But tonight feels different.

I can't let go of Sasha's words. I keep replaying her poem in my mind, trying to recall the exact phrasing and the rhythm of her voice as she spoke. Her words were like glass —delicate but powerful, fragile but cutting. She talked about walls, about love breaking us and rebuilding us, and there was something so raw, so intimate in the way she shared that part of herself. It wasn't just the poem itself; it was the way she delivered it, the way her voice trembled ever so slightly at the beginning but grew stronger with each line.

I wish I had the paper in front of me now, wish I could trace the ink with my fingertips and memorize every word. I want to hold onto it, to keep it close, to let it wash over me again and again. But more than that, I want to hold onto how she made me feel. There was something electric between us, something I haven't felt in a long time. It was like being struck by lightning, the intensity of it both exhilarating and terrifying. I've spent so long keeping my heart guarded, afraid of letting anyone in again, but with Sasha, those walls I've built feel like they're crumbling. And for the first time, I'm not trying to stop them from falling.

I roll over onto my side, pressing my cheek into the cool pillowcase. My thoughts keep drifting back to the way Sasha looked tonight: her dark hair falling in loose waves around her face and her lips curving into that soft, almost shy smile whenever she caught me looking at her. She was confident on stage, but there was also a vulnerability there, something that drew me in even more.

I close my eyes, trying to push the thoughts away, but instead, they intensify. I imagine what it would be like to kiss her, to feel her lips against mine, soft and warm. The thought sends a shiver down my spine, and I feel a heat building low in my stomach. It's been so long since I've let myself want someone like this, but with Sasha, the desire is undeniable, almost overwhelming. I can't stop thinking about her—about the way her skin might feel beneath my fingertips, the way her body might move under mine.

I let out a slow breath, my heart beating faster as the images in my mind take over. I imagine running my hands through her hair, feeling its softness, tugging her closer until our lips meet. I wonder what it would be like to taste her, to let my tongue trace the curve of her lips before deepening the kiss. The thought sends another rush of warmth through me, and I shift slightly in bed, trying to find a more comfortable position as the tension coils tighter inside me.

I can almost feel her now—her breath against my skin, the warmth of her body pressed against mine. The thought is intoxicating, and I can't help but let my mind wander further. I imagine the feel of her beneath me, her skin smooth and soft, her body arching as I kiss her neck, her collarbone, trailing my lips lower until I find the places that make her gasp.

My breath quickens as I think about how she would taste, how her skin would feel warm and sweet against my tongue. I can see it so clearly in my mind—Sasha, lying beneath me, her chest rising and falling with each breath, her eyes half-closed in pleasure. I can hear the soft sound of her moans, feel the way her body would respond to my touch, the way her fingers would dig into my skin as she pulls me closer.

The thought is almost too much to bear, and I can feel the heat pooling between my thighs, the need building in intensity. But it's not just physical. It's something deeper than that—something emotional, something that scares me, even as it draws me in. I want to touch her, yes, but more than that, I want to know her. I want to explore the parts of her that she's kept hidden, to uncover the things that make her who she is. I want to understand the way her mind works, to trace the lines of her thoughts like I would trace the lines of her body.

I open my eyes, staring into the darkness of my room. My heart is still racing, my skin tingling with anticipation, but there's a sense of calm beneath it all. It's strange, this feeling, this mix of desire and something else, something softer and more vulnerable. I've spent so long avoiding intimacy, so long keeping myself closed off from the possibility of love, but with Sasha, it feels different. It feels like maybe, just maybe, I'm ready to let someone in again.

I can't stop thinking about her—about the way her eyes lit up when we talked, about the way she listened so intently, like every word I said mattered. I've never met someone who made me feel so seen, so understood, and it's both thrilling and terrifying.

My fingers graze my lips as I imagine kissing her again, the softness of her mouth against mine, the way her breath would hitch as our bodies pressed closer. I want to touch her, to taste her, to feel the heat of her skin against mine.

I let out a soft sigh, rolling onto my back and staring up at the ceiling once again. The tension in my body hasn't lessened, but there's a peace that comes with it now—a sense of rightness, of inevitability. Whatever this is between us, it feels like something worth pursuing, something worth risking my heart for. And that's not a feeling I've had in a long time.

As my mind drifts further, I can't help but wonder what tomorrow will bring. We're meeting for coffee, but I already know it's going to be more than that. There's a connection between us, something unspoken but undeniable, and I'm ready to see where it leads. I'm ready to let myself feel again, to let myself want again. And for the first time in years, I'm not afraid of the possibility of getting hurt.

I close my eyes, letting the warmth of the sheets cocoon me as sleep begins to pull me under. But even as I drift off, my thoughts remain on her and the way she made me feel tonight. The way she made me feel seen, understood, desired. I fall asleep dreaming of her, of her lips on mine, of her skin beneath my hands, of the way her body might taste, warm and sweet against my tongue.

And as I slip into sleep, I know one thing for sure: This is just the beginning.

∼

"And that's exactly why I can't stand him," Sasha says with a grin, her eyes sparkling with mischief as she takes a sip of her coffee.

I can't help but laugh, shaking my head in disbelief. "You're kidding, right? How can you not love Walt Whitman? The man practically reinvented poetry!"

Sasha leans back, a sly smile pulling at her lips. "Oh, come on. He's a little too self-indulgent for my taste. All that 'Song of Myself' stuff—it's like, we get it, Walt. You really like yourself."

I feign shock, putting a hand over my heart. "Take that back! 'Song of Myself' is brilliant! It's about the universal human experience, the connection between all of us."

Sasha arches an eyebrow, clearly enjoying this. "Or it's just one long love letter to himself. Seriously, Evie, the man wrote an entire collection called *Leaves of Grass*. That's not just a poet; that's someone who spends way too much time admiring himself in the mirror."

I laugh again, shaking my head as I lean forward. "You are impossible. Fine, if you want to dismiss one of the greatest American poets, that's on you. But at least tell me you don't have the same problem with Sylvia Plath."

Sasha smirks, leaning in as if she's about to reveal some big secret. "Oh, Sylvia. Now there's someone who knew how to write about the dark stuff. But—"

I gasp, cutting her off. "But?"

Sasha raises a finger, pretending to be serious. "Hear me out. I love Sylvia Plath, I really do. But sometimes...don't you think she's a little too bleak? Like, I get it, life sucks, but does it have to suck that much?"

I let out a dramatic sigh, leaning back in my chair. "Sasha, you're killing me here. Plath is all about raw emotion. She doesn't sugarcoat anything, and that's what makes her work so powerful. It's unfiltered; it's honest. It's human."

Sasha chuckles softly, clearly enjoying herself. "I'm not denying that. I just think, maybe, just maybe, a little bit of light at the end of the tunnel wouldn't hurt."

I can't help but laugh at that, shaking my head as I sip my coffee. "Okay, fine. If Plath is too bleak for you, who's your go-to poet? The one who gets it just right?"

Without hesitation, Sasha answers, "Maya Angelou. Hands down."

I nod, relief washing over me. "Finally, we agree on something. Maya is a goddess."

"Right?!" Sasha's face lights up, her hands gesturing excitedly. "She has this perfect blend of strength and vulnerability. She writes about pain, but she also writes about resilience. 'Still I Rise?' That poem is a masterpiece."

I smile, leaning in a bit closer. "And the way she uses rhythm and repetition, it's like her words stick with you, like a melody you can't get out of your head."

Sasha leans forward too, lowering her voice like she's

about to share a secret. "Did you know she was also a calypso singer? I mean, seriously, is there anything she couldn't do?"

My eyes widen in surprise. "Wait, I didn't know that! She was a singer?"

Sasha nods, grinning. "Yep. She had a whole career before she became a writer. She even recorded an album."

I shake my head, laughing softly. "That woman was unstoppable."

We both settle back in our chairs, taking a moment to enjoy our coffees, and there's this quiet comfort between us, like we've known each other for far longer than we have. But then, Sasha grins again, mischief flashing in her eyes.

"Okay," she says, setting her cup down with a satisfied look. "So we're on the same page with Maya Angelou. But what about prose? Tell me you're not one of those people who's obsessed with James Joyce."

I groan, rolling my eyes. "Oh god, Joyce. Don't even get me started. *Ulysses* is like the literary equivalent of torture. Sure, it's impressive, but who actually enjoys reading it?"

Sasha bursts out laughing, nodding in agreement. "Exactly! It's like, 'Congratulations, you read 700 pages of stream-of-consciousness nonsense. Here's a migraine for your efforts.'"

I nearly spit out my coffee from laughing so hard that I have to set the cup down. "Yes! I've tried to read it three times, and every time I end up questioning my life choices."

Sasha wipes away a tear from laughing so hard. "See? You get it. People only pretend to like it because it makes them sound smart."

I raise my cup, still laughing. "To the truth. We're just here for the good stories, not to impress anyone."

Sasha grins and clinks her cup against mine. "Cheers to that."

The conversation flows effortlessly. We start trading stories about the authors we love and the ones we just can't stand, laughing so hard at times that the baristas shoot us a few amused glances. Sasha and I talk over each other constantly, each of us building off the other's ideas, the banter sharp and quick but always playful.

"Okay," I say, leaning forward with a grin. "Serious question: Austen or Brontë?"

Sasha raises an eyebrow and pretends to think deeply, tapping her chin dramatically. "Hmm, that's a tough one. Austen is the queen of witty dialogue, but Brontë, she's got that whole dark, brooding, Byronic hero thing going on."

I nod, a playful smile tugging at my lips. "True. But I'll take Mr. Darcy's smoldering looks over Heathcliff's tortured soul any day."

Sasha snorts, covering her mouth to hide her laugh. "Darcy is the original 'tall, dark, and handsome,' but let's be real, he's kind of a jerk at first. Elizabeth Bennet had to do some serious emotional labor there."

I laugh, shaking my head. "But that's what makes it satisfying! She puts him in his place, and he actually grows as a person. Heathcliff, on the other hand, is just…irredeemable."

Sasha concedes with a nod. "Okay, fair point. But if we're talking dark and brooding, Brontë still wins."

We both laugh, settling into the kind of conversation that feels like a dance—fluid, energetic, full of unexpected turns but always in rhythm. We challenge each other's opinions, but there's no edge to it. It's all in good fun, and every time Sasha counters one of my points, I can't help but admire her quick wit.

Time passes without us noticing, the light outside shifting from late afternoon to evening. It is a good thing I left Ken manning the desk. He is closer to eighty than he would ever admit, but he happily covers the counter when I need a break.

The coffee shop has grown quieter now that most of the customers are gone, and the baristas are starting to clean up around us. But Sasha and I are still locked in conversation, our cups long since emptied, but neither of us ready to end the moment.

Her green eyes are sparkling and I can't tear my gaze away from them.

I look at my watch and let out a soft laugh. "We've been here for hours. I think the baristas are ready to kick us out."

Sasha chuckles, glancing around the nearly empty shop. "Yeah, I think we might've overstayed our welcome. But this was really fun."

I smile, feeling a warmth spread through my chest. "It was. I can't remember the last time I had a conversation like this."

Sasha looks at me, her eyes softening for just a moment, and then she grins again. "Well, you better get used to it because I've got a lot more opinions to share."

I laugh, shaking my head. "I'm looking forward to it."

As we stand and gather our things, there's a quiet understanding between us. This isn't the end of our conversation; it's just the beginning. And I can't help but feel excited about what's to come.

We walk to the door, still talking and laughing, and for the first time in a long while, I feel like I've found something special.

As we step out into the cool evening air, the playful banter between us begins to taper off, replaced by a sudden, quiet awareness of the moment. The sounds of the city hum around us—distant streetcars clattering, a soft breeze rustling through the nearby trees, and the occasional laughter of people passing by—but it all feels muted. Like the world has faded into the background, leaving just the two of us standing there, inches apart.

I tuck my hair behind my ear, feeling the familiar awkwardness creep in as the conversation lulls. This is the part I'm never good at: the ending. I don't know if I should hug her, shake her hand, or just wave awkwardly and make a quick escape. My mind starts to race through all the possibilities, and suddenly, I'm hyper-aware of how close we're standing.

Sasha is still looking at me, her lips curved into that soft, teasing smile that I've grown so fond of in just a short amount of time. But there's something else in her beautiful green eyes now—something deeper, more intense. It sends a little thrill through me, and I feel my heart rate pick up and my breath catch in my throat.

"Well," I start, my voice a little shaky despite my best effort to sound casual, "this was really nice. I had a great time."

Sasha doesn't say anything at first. She just watches me, her eyes flicking over my face, taking in every detail. Her smile fades slightly, replaced by a more serious expression that makes my stomach flip with anticipation.

"I did too," she finally says, her voice low and soft. She steps a little closer, her presence warm in the cool air.

There's a moment of silence, one of those charged pauses that makes the air between us feel thick with possibility. My mind is racing, trying to figure out what to do next. Should I just leave? Should I say something?

But then Sasha makes the decision for me.

Before I can overthink it any further, she closes the small distance between us. Her hand finds its way to the back of my neck, her fingers threading gently through my hair. There's no hesitation in her movement, no awkward fumbling. Just a quiet confidence that makes my breath hitch.

And then, before I can even process what's happening, her lips are on mine.

The kiss is soft at first—gentle, almost testing—but there's an underlying intensity that makes my whole body tingle with warmth. My initial shock melts away almost instantly, and I find myself leaning into her, my hand instinctively reaching for her waist, pulling her closer.

Everything I had imagined alone could never have prepared me for the real thing.

Sasha's lips are warm and soft against mine, and the world around us seems to disappear entirely. There's nothing but the feel of her mouth moving against mine, the way her breath mingles with mine, the way her hand tightens ever so slightly in my hair. It's like the tension that's been building between us has finally snapped, and all I can do is give in to the pull.

I lose myself in the kiss, letting it deepen as my hands slide up to her shoulders, my fingers pressing into the soft fabric of her jacket. She responds in kind, her other hand slipping around my waist, pulling me closer until there's barely any space between us. The kiss grows more intense, more urgent, and I can feel the heat building between us, the electricity crackling in the air.

It's everything I didn't know I wanted.

When we finally pull away, breathless and a little dazed, we're both smiling—soft, nervous smiles that betray the excitement still buzzing between us. My heart is racing, my cheeks flushed, and for a moment, all I can do is stare at her, my mind still trying to catch up to what just happened.

Sasha's eyes are locked on mine, her hand still resting gently on the back of my neck, her thumb brushing the edge of my hairline. She looks just as breathless as I feel, her lips slightly swollen from the kiss, her gaze heavy with something that makes my heart skip.

"I've been wanting to do that all day," she says softly, her voice a little husky, a playful smile tugging at the corner of her mouth.

I laugh softly, biting my lip as I look up at her. "I'm glad you did."

8

SASHA

My lips are still tingling, and my mind is spinning from the kiss. It's as if the rest of the world has melted away, leaving just Evie and me suspended in this perfect, breathless moment. I pull back slowly, feeling her warm breath against my skin, and I can't help but smile at the way her dark eyes are still half-closed, dazed and a little shy, like she's as surprised by this as I am.

We're both quiet for a second, the sounds of the city faintly buzzing around us, but neither of us seems ready to step back into reality. I'm usually not the type to get swept up in things so quickly, but with Evie, it's like all the rules I've made for myself don't matter. All I want is more—more of her smile, her touch, this feeling that's buzzing between us.

I clear my throat, trying to sound casual even though my heart is still racing. "So, this was not how I thought today was going to go," I say with a half-laugh, my voice a little shaky with leftover adrenaline.

Evie laughs softly, biting her lip as she meets my gaze. "Me neither," she admits, her cheeks flushed in a way that makes her look even more beautiful than she did a moment ago. There's something so real and unguarded about her in this moment, and it makes my chest ache with a kind of sweet, unexpected longing.

I don't want this to end. Not yet.

"Well, if you're not ready to call it a night..." I choose my words carefully. I don't want to come on too strong, but the thought of saying goodbye right now feels impossible. "I mean, no pressure or anything, but if you want to...we could go back to my place for a bit? Just hang out. No expectations."

I catch the flicker of something in her eyes—surprise, excitement, maybe even a little hesitation. It's clear she's tempted, and that alone is enough to make my heart skip a beat.

She looks at me, her lips curling into a soft, thoughtful smile. "I'd like that," she says, her voice gentle, almost tentative. "But"—she glances down at her watch, the briefest shadow of responsibility crossing her face—"I need to go back to the bookstore first. I kind of left things unfinished, and Kenneth's probably waiting for me to close up."

I nod, trying to hide my disappointment, but there's no real sting to it. It's just a delay, a small bump in the road. "Yeah, of course," I say, keeping my tone light. "I get it. Responsible bookstore owner duties and all."

"But you could come with me to lock up, and then we could go after?" she asks a little cautiously, and I nod, a smile spreading.

She smiles at that, relaxing a little, and we start walking back together, falling into an easy rhythm. The anticipation is still buzzing between us, every step feeling like it's filled with possibility.

We're not saying it out loud, but it's there in every glance, every accidental brush of our hands as we walk side by side. I've never felt this pulled toward someone so quickly, but with Evie, it's like every moment is an invitation to something deeper.

As we get closer, I can feel the anticipation building, a quiet buzz that seems to settle between every word we say. I glance at her, catching the way her eyes flick toward me when she thinks I'm not looking, and it sends a rush of heat to my cheeks. There's something so genuine about the way she looks at me, like she's trying to figure out what's happening between us but is just as caught up in it as I am.

The bookstore comes into view, its familiar silhouette warmly lit from within, and I can already see Kenneth moving about, tidying up the last few things. The place looks cozy and inviting, but there's something different about it tonight. Maybe it's knowing that Evie and I will be alone soon and that this space that's so uniquely hers will be ours for just a little while.

Evie opens the door and we step inside, the bell above the door jingling softly. The bookstore feels different at this hour—quieter, like it's holding its breath, waiting for whatever's going to happen next. The smell of old paper and polished wood wraps around us, familiar and comforting, but there's an edge of something more: a sense of private intimacy that wasn't there earlier.

Kenneth looks up, giving us both a friendly smile. He's an older man who doesn't miss the way we keep glancing at each other or the lingering tension that neither of us is bothering to hide.

"Hey, boss," Kenneth says with a little wink. "You're back early. Or should I say back just in time to kick me out."

Evie laughs, shaking her head as she moves behind the counter, her movements quick and practiced. "Sorry, Kenneth. I think I'm going to close a little early tonight. Thanks for holding down the fort."

Kenneth gives her a knowing smile then glances at me, his eyes twinkling with amusement. "No problem at all. You two have a good night." He waves as he grabs his jacket and makes his way to the door without asking any questions. I get the feeling he's seen more than his fair share of late-night bookstore closings that have nothing to do with books.

As soon as the door shuts behind him, the atmosphere shifts again. It's just the two of us now, and the bookstore feels almost sacred, like it's wrapped us in a secret we haven't quite spoken aloud. Evie moves around the space with a quiet confidence, checking the register and tidying up stray books, but there's a new tension in the air—one that makes every second feel heavy with possibility.

I watch her, captivated by the way she handles everything so effortlessly, so naturally. There's something incredibly attractive about seeing her in her element, the way her fingers brush over the spines of books and the way she moves like she's perfectly at home in every corner of this place. I lean against one of the bookshelves, trying to keep my cool, but it's hard when my heart is beating this fast.

My eyes glance over her body, the beautiful curve of her ass in her jeans. The lovely hint of her line of her breasts in her loose fitting shirt and a flash of her stomach as she reaches up to place one book back on a high shelf.

Evie catches me watching her, and she pauses, a shy smile tugging at her lips. "Sorry, I'm almost done," she says, her voice soft and a little breathless. "I know this probably isn't the most exciting way to spend the evening."

"Are you kidding?" I push off the shelf and move closer, close enough that I can feel the warmth radiating from her. "I think this is pretty perfect."

She smiles, her eyes lingering on mine a little longer this time, and there's a moment, a single beat, where everything seems to slow. The register clicks shut, the last light flickers off, and Evie moves to the door, turning the lock with a soft, deliberate click. The sound echoes in the quiet, and when she turns back to me, it's like all the tension we've been dancing around suddenly breaks free.

We were supposed to be leaving, but all I can think about is how much I want to kiss her again. The air between us feels charged, electric, and I can't hold back any longer. I step closer, my breath hitching as I reach for her, my fingers brushing lightly against her arm. Evie looks up at me, her eyes wide and dark, and for a split second, I think we might actually make it out the door.

But then, before either of us can think too much about it, our lips meet again. It's soft at first, a tentative kiss that quickly deepens, fueled by everything we've been holding back. There's no hesitation this time, no awkwardness—just a desperate need to feel more of each other, to close every inch of space between us.

We're kissing like the world outside doesn't exist, like the only thing that matters is this moment right here in the dim light of the bookstore. My hands find their way into her hair, pulling her closer, and Evie's hands grip my waist, tugging me against her like she can't get close enough.

We are supposed to be leaving. But right now, neither of us can seem to let go.

It starts slow. We've been slow all day—careful touches,

playful glances, hours of dancing around the edge of something we both want but haven't quite let ourselves take. But now, as our lips meet in the dim light of the bookstore, there's no holding back.

I kiss her softly at first, testing, tasting, savoring the moment. But there's a simmering urgency beneath it all, a feeling that's been building since the coffee shop and our first kiss on the street, and now it's finally breaking free. The bookstore is dim and quiet; the only sounds are the faint hum of the city outside and the soft, almost desperate sighs that escape between us.

Evie's lips are warm and insistent, and I can feel the shift in her body as she presses into me, her hands sliding around my back, pulling me closer. We're moving against the door, my back against the cool glass, but even that feels distant compared to the heat of her mouth on mine. I grab at her waist, fingers curling into the fabric of her sweater, but she takes control, pushing me harder against the door, her mouth claiming mine with a new intensity that makes me gasp.

She pins me there, her hands framing my face, and there's something so intoxicating about the way she looks at me, like I'm the only thing that matters. But the moment doesn't stay slow for long. The restraint we've held onto all day snaps, and before I can even think, we're shifting, moving, and reversing positions until it's Evie's back against the shelves, her body arching into mine as I press into her.

My hands are everywhere—on her waist, tangled in her hair, slipping beneath her sweater to feel the soft, heated skin underneath. She gasps at my touch, her breath catching, and it's like a switch flips. We go from tentative to desperate in seconds, our mouths clashing in a kiss that's all teeth and hunger, pulling at each other's lips, scraping, biting, needing.

Evie moans softly as I push her further against the shelves, and a few books tumble to the floor, forgotten. My fingers trace the curve of her spine, pulling her closer, and she grabs at my shirt, her hands slipping under the fabric, her cool fingertips dragging over my skin. I can feel the heat rising between us, the air thick and heavy. The AC has turned off along with the rest of the lights, making the room feel even hotter, more suffocating in the best possible way.

I pull away just long enough to meet her gaze, and the look in her eyes—dark, intense, filled with the same raw need that's burning inside me—makes my knees weak. There's nothing tentative now, no space for second-guessing or hesitation. I press my body into hers, feeling the full length of her against me, and it's like every nerve ending is on fire, desperate for more.

Evie pushes back, turning the tables, and suddenly I'm the one pinned against the shelves, my breath hitching as her hands roam over my sides, slipping under my shirt and grazing the bare skin beneath. Her lips find mine again, more insistent this time, and I bite down softly on her lower lip, pulling, teasing, feeling her shudder against me. The sound she makes—a low, needy moan—sends a jolt of heat straight through me.

The kiss turns frantic, almost animalistic, as if we've been starving for this and can't get enough. My hands slide up her sweater, pushing it higher until my fingertips brush the curve of her ribs, and she arches into me, gasping as our bodies press closer. The space around us seems to shrink, the shelves digging into my back as she kisses me like she's trying to consume me, and I want it. I want all of it, all of her.

We're moving around the store, tangled together, knocking books off the shelves in our wake. Evie's hands are pulling at my clothes, and I'm doing the same, fingers fumbling at the hem of her sweater, tugging it up and over her head, the fabric catching briefly on her hair before it falls to the floor. I push her back, this time against a sturdy table covered in a stack of old paperbacks, and she gasps, the sound echoing softly in the otherwise quiet room.

Her hands find the waistband of my jeans, yanking me closer, and I nearly lose my balance, the rush of it all making me dizzy. But I don't care; I'm past caring. I just want her and she wants me, and we're moving so fast but it still doesn't feel like enough.

Evie's lips are on my neck, her teeth grazing the sensitive skin there, and I gasp, my head falling back as I grip the edge of the table to steady myself. She's relentless, her mouth hot against my throat, nipping and kissing her way down, and I can feel my own control slipping with every touch, every desperate tug of my clothes.

My fingers fan across the table, holding myself up as she moves down my body. My jeans are tight, and I curse them. They look good on my ass, but what I would give for a quick pull and for them to be gone. But Evie just grins up at me as she lowers onto her knees, savoring the time it takes, each slow second of peeling them from my skin. She kisses down my body, over my panties, thighs, knees, shins, and as my foot rises, even my ankle gets a soft kiss too. And that makes me lose my mind. I let out a low moan because who knew it could be just so fucking sexy.

Then she makes me suffer every slow second again on her way back up. It is agonizing. I can feel the wetness spread through my panties. They're soaked through, and I would be embarrassed by my need if I had any time to process my thoughts. She is so close, and her nose brushes over the fabric as her lips reach my upper thigh. I feel her inhale, smelling me, taking me in. Like I can have no secrets from her, she even takes my scent.

And with the slowest of pulls, she peels down the silk of my panties. I think she will wait, and I brace myself, tensing every muscle, but she reads my body, knows I am there, that I have waited long enough, and she buries her face against my pussy. A deep suck, a push and swirl of her tongue, instant pressure. Her hands take my hips and rock them so I'm on her tongue. To say it takes seconds for me to come would be an exaggeration. I let it all out, right there in the middle of the store against her beautiful face, my need and desire leaving a glossy sheen on her skin as I moan and writhe over and over, completely lost in her. One bit of pressure from her tongue was all it took- as though we were made for each other. My orgasm has no control, no restraint, and she is so hungry for it all.

For a moment, there's nothing but the pounding of my heart, the raw, electric pulse of pleasure still echoing through my veins. I cling to Evie, trying to catch my breath, my body feeling both impossibly light and achingly heavy, like I might float away if not for the steady, grounding presence of her arms around me. My mind is blissfully blank, filled only with the fading waves of everything she's just pulled out of me.

Evie pulls back slightly, just enough to look at me, her breath still warm against my skin. The way she looks at me —soft, tender, with a kind of quiet intensity—makes my chest ache. It's a look that says so much more than words ever could, and I can feel the weight of it settling over me like a blanket, wrapping me up in this sudden, unexpected tenderness.

She leans in, brushing her lips against my temple in a kiss that's so gentle, so careful, it makes my eyes sting. Her mouth lingers there, and I let out a slow, shuddering breath, feeling that kiss seep into me, grounding me, anchoring me.

Without speaking, Evie takes my hand, her fingers curling around mine as she gently guides me down to the floor, right there among the scattered books. I follow, still dazed, still floating somewhere between reality and this dreamlike state where nothing else matters but the two of us. I feel the lingering warmth of release in my limbs, a pleasant heaviness that makes every movement slow and deliberate.

Evie settles us on the floor, carefully maneuvering around the paperbacks. Her movements are slow and tender, like she's handling something fragile, and there's a kind of reverence in the way she touches me, like she's trying to hold onto the moment just as tightly as I am. She reaches for a blanket that's draped over one of the chairs and wraps it around us, pulling me close until we're cocooned together in the quiet, messy intimacy of this space.

I melt into her, resting my cheek against her chest, and the sound of her heartbeat is like a lullaby, soft and rhythmic, soothing every part of me that's still buzzing with leftover adrenaline. I listen to it and let it wash over me, and for the first time in what feels like forever, I feel safe. I feel sated, content, wrapped up in something that feels bigger than just this moment.

Evie's arms come around me, holding me tight, and I let myself relax into her completely. The bookstore is quiet around us, the soft rustle of the blanket the only sound breaking the stillness. I can't remember the last time I let myself feel this—this kind of calm, this closeness. I don't want to move, don't want to do anything but stay wrapped up in Evie, feeling the warmth of her body against mine, the comforting weight of the blanket over us.

I feel tears forming in the corners of my eyes.

We don't need to speak. The silence says everything. And I feel like I'm exactly where I'm meant to be.

9

EVIE

The bookstore is still bathed in the soft blue light of early morning when I wake up, and for a moment, I'm disoriented, caught between the fading dream of last night and reality slowly coming into focus. I can feel the familiar, comforting weight of the bookstore around me —the scent of old paper, the quiet hum of the city outside— but there's something different, something warmer, more immediate.

It's Sasha. She's curled up beside me, still tangled in the blanket we pulled off the chair last night, her hair spilling over her face in messy waves. Her breathing is soft and even, the rise and fall of her chest a quiet rhythm that matches the peaceful calm I feel settling in my own chest. I watch her for a moment, feeling the warmth of her body against mine, and it hits me all over again: She's here, we're here, and everything that happened last night wasn't just some vivid, fleeting dream.

My mind drifts back to last night—kisses that grew hungrier, touches that lingered longer, and the way we'd finally given in, losing ourselves in the messy, beautiful chaos of each other. The bookstore is still a little wrecked from it: books scattered across the floor, a couple of chairs tipped sideways, and the faintest hint of our laughter still echoed in the corners. It's never felt more like my space, yet also, for the first time, like something shared.

I take a slow breath, feeling the cool air against my skin where the blanket doesn't quite reach, and I let myself relax into the moment. Sasha stirs beside me, her eyes fluttering open, and when she looks up at me, there's this soft, sleepy smile that tugs at my heart.

"Morning," she murmurs, her voice husky and warm, still heavy with sleep.

"Morning," I whisper back, my fingers reaching out to brush a strand of hair away from her face. The gesture feels natural, easy, and Sasha leans into it, her bright green eyes closing briefly as if savoring the touch.

There's a comfortable silence that stretches between us, filled with the quiet sounds of the world waking up outside. I've never been good at mornings—too many thoughts crashing in at once, too many things to do—but right now, all I want is to stay here, wrapped up in this rare feeling of peace.

But the day is already creeping in, and as much as I want to linger in this bubble, there's a bookstore to run. I sit up slowly, stretch my arms above my head, and glance around at the scattered books, the disarray that marks our path from last night. It's a mess, but it's our mess, and that thought brings a small, unexpected smile to my lips.

"We really did a number on the place, huh?" Sasha says, her voice laced with amusement as she follows my gaze, taking in the aftermath of our evening.

I chuckle, nodding as I stand, offering her my hand to

pull her up beside me. "Yeah, I don't think I've ever seen it like this. But hey, it's kind of a look, don't you think?"

Sasha laughs softly, and the sound is like music easing the last of the tension from my shoulders. We start to move around the bookstore, picking up books and righting chairs, slipping easily into a rhythm that feels like we've done this a hundred times before. It's not awkward; it's strangely comfortable, like we've found a new way of fitting into each other's lives, even in the quiet routines of the morning.

She reaches for a stack of books near the counter, pausing to read a few of the titles before carefully placing them back on the shelf. I watch her, captivated by the simple way she moves, her focus so genuine, like she's savoring every small detail. There's something incredibly intimate about seeing her like this—in my space, handling my books, bringing her presence into the nooks and crannies of my life.

As we work, we fall into easy conversation, punctuated by soft laughter and the occasional teasing remark. She makes fun of my alphabetized shelves, and I roll my eyes, defending my organizational system with mock seriousness. There's a lightness to it all, a playful back-and-forth that feels like we've known each other much longer than we have. It's a new kind of intimacy, not just in touch, but in the way we talk, the way we share the space, the way her presence blends seamlessly into my morning routine.

I catch her watching me a few times, her gaze lingering in a way that makes my skin warm. There's a quiet intensity, like she's memorizing every detail, and it makes my heart stutter. I realize I'm doing the same—watching her move, listening to the cadence of her voice, holding onto every little moment because it feels too good to let slip away.

Eventually, the bookstore is back in order, but it doesn't feel the same. It feels new, like it's been touched by something I didn't know I needed. I turn back to Sasha, wiping my hands on my jeans and smiling softly as she looks at me, and for a second, everything else falls away. The morning light filters through the windows, casting soft shadows across the shelves, and there's a feeling in the air that I can't quite name but don't want to lose.

She steps closer, reaching out to brush her fingers against mine, and it's such a small, simple touch, but it makes my chest tighten. "I like this," she says quietly, her voice gentle. "Being here with you. It feels...right."

I squeeze her hand, feeling a swell of warmth that starts in my chest and spreads through my whole body. "Yeah," I whisper, my smile widening. "It really does."

"But"—her voice is filled with an unexpected seriousness, and I feel my heart stop a second, a crash of reality feeling imminent—"it is seriously lacking in coffee."

And she kisses me before I can let out the breath I am holding.

～

The morning stretches longer than I expect, but I don't mind. Every second with Sasha feels like it's bending time, making it feel richer, fuller, like it's worth more. But now, reality is starting to seep back in. The sun is rising higher, casting soft, golden light through the windows, and the city outside is coming to life. Sasha glances at her phone, her expression softening with a hint of reluctance. It's a look I know all too well; the one that says, "I'd stay if I could." She has things to do, a life beyond this morning, and I feel the inevitable pull of time tugging at the edges of our little cocoon.

She catches my eye, and I see the same bittersweet mix of contentment and hesitation reflecting back at me. We've spent hours together—talking, laughing, getting lost in each other—and yet it feels like not nearly enough. She's still holding a book she picked up earlier, her fingers tracing the spine absentmindedly as she smiles at me, and the sight of it makes my chest tighten with a strange, unexpected ache.

"I should probably get going," Sasha says softly, her voice tinged with the faintest trace of regret. "I've got a shift at the wing bar later, and I should probably try to look somewhat presentable."

I nod, trying to muster a smile that doesn't feel like goodbye. "Of course. And I've got...well, the bookstore, obviously." I gesture vaguely toward the shelves and the half-finished coffee cups on the counter, the quiet space that's suddenly starting to feel a little too empty.

She moves closer, setting the book back on the shelf, and it takes all my willpower not to reach out and pull her back into me. Her presence feels so natural here, like she's always been a part of this place, and the thought of her leaving now feels like waking up from a dream I'm not ready to let go of.

"Last night was..." Her voice trails off as she searches for the right words. She shakes her head, a small, almost shy smile breaking through. "Well, you know."

I laugh softly, nodding as I lean against the counter, trying to keep my composure. "Yeah. I know."

There's a pause, a soft, lingering silence where neither of us seems to want to move. I watch her, taking in every little detail: the way her hair falls casually over her shoulder, the curve of her smile, the light in her eyes that still feels like it's holding on to me. I don't want this to be the last time I see that look, the last time I feel this warmth that's been wrapping itself around my heart all morning.

But then Sasha reaches out, her fingers brushing mine in a touch so gentle it almost breaks me. "This isn't the end of this, right?" she asks, her voice soft but certain, like she's already decided the answer. "I mean, I'd like to see you again. Soon."

There's a flutter in my chest, a rush of something I haven't felt in a long time: hope. I nod, squeezing her hand just a little tighter. "Yeah. I'd like that too."

She smiles, and it's like the sun coming up all over again. I watch as she turns toward the door, her steps slow and reluctant, like she's feeling the same pull I am. I want to say something, to find the perfect words to capture everything that's buzzing inside me, but they all feel too big for this quiet morning moment. So I let her go, my eyes following her as she steps out onto the sidewalk, the bell above the door chiming softly behind her.

The door closes, and suddenly, it's just me and the bookstore. The quiet is different now, filled with the echo of her laughter, the memory of her touch, and the lingering warmth of the hours we spent wrapped up in each other. I run my fingers over the counter where she stood, tracing the spot where her hand had rested, and I can still feel the faint, comforting imprint of her presence.

I move through the bookstore, straightening a few books that are still slightly out of place, and I can't help but smile. It's a small thing, this rearranging of shelves, but it feels like putting something back together that's been waiting to be whole. The space feels more alive than it ever has, like it's holding onto the energy Sasha brought with her, and I want more of it—more of her, more of this feeling that's still humming in my veins.

I take a deep breath, letting the air settle in my lungs, and as I turn back to the front of the store, I feel a flicker of excitement, the kind that only comes when something new is beginning. This morning wasn't just a moment; it was a promise, one that whispers quietly between us, even now that she's gone.

I don't know what comes next, but for once, I'm not afraid of the unknown. I'm ready to see where this takes us, ready to open up to the possibility of something real. And as I flip the sign on the door to "Open," I can't help but smile.

10

SASHA

The walk back to my apartment is a blur, the morning light just starting to filter through the buildings and paint everything in a soft, golden hue. I'm still riding the high of last night, of Evie's touch, her warmth, the way we fit together like something inevitable. Every step feels lighter, and I'm grinning like an idiot, replaying every kiss, every stolen moment between the shelves.

I can't remember the last time I felt this good, this...alive. But as I turn the corner to my building, reality nudges back in, reminding me of the world beyond the quiet, intimate bubble of Evie's bookstore. And there, leaning casually against the entrance, is Glass, his lanky frame draped in one of his usual oversized sweaters, a coffee cup in one hand and a knowing smirk already forming on his lips.

He looks up as I approach, and his smile widens. "Well, well, well," he drawls, raising the coffee in a mock toast. "If it isn't my wayward friend, fresh from a night of...not sleeping in her own bed."

I roll my eyes, trying to keep my cool, but there's no

point pretending I'm not totally caught. "Good morning to you too, Sherlock," I shoot back, reaching out to swipe the coffee from his hand. I take a sip, savoring the familiar bitterness, and then glance at him with mock annoyance. "What are you doing lurking around my building this early?"

Glass chuckles, watching me with an expression that's far too amused for this time of day. "Oh, you know, just waiting to catch a glimpse of my favorite runaway poet. And look at that, I get more than I bargained for." He gestures to me, his eyes sweeping over my rumpled clothes and barely tamed mess of my hair, and I know I must look like someone who didn't plan to spend the night out.

I shake my head, unable to keep the grin off my face. "I'm not a runaway."

Glass arches an eyebrow, the smirk still firmly in place. "Really? Because from where I'm standing, you look like someone who's run straight into trouble. Or something like it."

I laugh, pushing past him toward the entrance, but Glass follows, still eyeing me with that infuriatingly perceptive look. He's been my best friend for years, long enough to know when something's different, when I'm hiding something. And right now, I'm not sure I want to hide this. Not from him.

"You're impossible, you know that?" I say, nudging the door open and holding it for him. He steps inside, and we both start up the stairs, his coffee still clutched in my hand.

"It's part of my charm," Glass replies, his voice light but probing. "So, are you going to tell me where you've been, or should I just start guessing?"

I hesitate for a second, biting my lip as I think about how much to share. But then I see the genuine curiosity in his eyes and the warmth that's always there no matter how much we tease each other, and I can't help but spill a little of the truth.

"I was with Evie Rousseau, the bookstore owner," I say, trying to sound casual, but even saying her name sends a little thrill through me. "We...I don't know. It just sort of happened. I went to her bookstore for the poetry night, and one thing led to another..."

Glass whistles low, shaking his head in mock amazement. "So the mysterious bookstore owner finally got you, huh? I knew there was something going on when you kept talking about her open mic like it was the highlight of your week."

I roll my eyes, but I can't deny it. "Yeah, well, she's...she's different. It feels different."

Glass gives me a knowing look, his smirk softening into something more genuine. "Good different?"

I nod, feeling my cheeks warm at the admission. "Yeah. Good different."

We reach my door, and I fumble with my keys, still buzzing with the residual energy of Evie, of the way her smile lingered in my mind as I left. I push the door open, and Glass follows me inside, tossing his bag onto the nearest chair and flopping down on the couch like he owns the place. I drop my bag next to his and collapse beside him, sinking into the familiar cushions with a tired but contented sigh.

"So," Glass says, turning to face me, his eyes sparkling with mischief, "tell me everything. Did you recite sonnets by candlelight? Spill wine on first editions? I need all the details."

I laugh, nudging him playfully. "You're not getting the full play-by-play, you perv. But...it was good. More than good, actually. It was—" I pause, searching for the right words, but all that comes to mind is Evie's touch, her laughter, the way her arms wrapped around me when the world finally quieted down. "It was...easy. And intense. And I don't know, it just felt right."

Glass watches me, his smirk giving way to a softer smile. "I'm glad. You deserve something that feels right, Sash."

I lean back, closing my eyes as I let the warmth of his words settle. There's a comfort in knowing that Glass gets it, that he's happy for me without needing every detail, without turning it into something bigger than it is. He's always been like that—supportive, steady, and a constant presence in the whirlwind of my life.

We sit in companionable silence for a few moments, sipping our coffee and letting the quiet morning unfold around us. My thoughts keep drifting back to Evie and the way she looked at me when I left, like there was more to say, more to explore. And even though we're apart now, I can still feel the pull of her, the promise of something new and unfamiliar but oh so enticing.

Glass nudges me with his elbow, breaking the quiet. "You gonna see her again?"

I nod, unable to hide the small, eager smile that spreads across my face. "Yeah. I think this is just the start."

Glass raises his coffee cup in a mock toast. "To new beginnings, then. And to you finally finding something worth sticking around for."

I clink my cup against his, feeling the warmth of his friendship settle around me like a second skin. It's comforting, grounding, and as I take another sip, I know one thing for sure: Whatever happens next with Evie, I'm ready for it.

∼

The familiar clatter of plates and the hum of conversation greet me as I step into the wing place, the late morning light filtering through the windows, casting a warm glow over the bustling restaurant. It's already busy—tables filled with regulars and the occasional new face, all of them eager for a good meal and a cold beer. The smells hit me immediately: the spicy tang of hot sauce, the rich scent of fried chicken, the comforting aroma of garlic and herbs. It's a sensory overload that wakes me up better than any cup of coffee could.

I slip behind the counter, grabbing my apron from the hook where I left it, and tie it around my waist with practiced ease. The fabric feels familiar against my fingers, worn soft from countless shifts. It's a simple ritual, one that always helps me switch gears and get into the right mindset for the busy day ahead.

"Morning, Sash," Jackson calls from the kitchen, his voice muffled by the sound of sizzling oil and the clatter of pans. He pops his head out, flashing me a grin. "You're in early. Thought you might be dragging your feet after a late night."

I give him a knowing smile, shaking my head. "Not a chance, boss. You know I'm always ready to work."

He laughs, a deep, hearty sound that echoes through the kitchen. "That's what I like to hear. We're slammed already, so it's good to have you on board."

I don't waste any time. The moment I hit the floor, I'm in motion—taking orders, refilling drinks, making small talk with the regulars who've come to know me as the friendly face who always remembers their favorite wing sauce. There's a rhythm to it, a steady pace that keeps me moving and focused. It's exactly what I need after the whirlwind of emotions from last night and this morning. No time to overthink, no time to dwell—just work.

The hours pass in a blur of activity. Plates are piled high with wings, fries, and all the fixings; drinks are poured and served with a smile; orders are taken and delivered with the same easy efficiency I've honed over countless shifts. I can feel the tiredness tugging at the edges of my energy, but it's a good kind of tiredness—the kind that comes from knowing you're doing something well, from the satisfaction of a job that keeps you on your toes.

The customers are in good spirits today, and so am I. I crack jokes with the regulars, tease the new customers about their wing choices, and make sure no one's glass stays empty for long. The tips start piling up, a few bills here and there, tucked into the pocket of my apron.

"Hey, Sasha," one of the regulars—Tommy, a guy who's been coming here for years—calls out as I pass by his table. "You look like you've had a good night. Got that glow about you."

I laugh, shaking my head as I refill his beer. "Just doing my job, Tommy. Maybe it's all the hot sauce fumes getting to me."

He grins, taking the fresh beer with a nod of thanks. "Whatever it is, keep it up. You're brightening up the place."

I flash him a quick smile and move on to the next table, the compliment lingering in the back of my mind like a warm ember. It's nice to be noticed, even in the small, casual ways that don't mean much beyond the moment.

As the lunch rush starts to wind down, I finally get a chance to catch my breath. I lean against the counter for a moment, stretching my arms above my head and rolling my shoulders to ease the tension. It's been non-stop since I walked in, but I can't say I mind. There's something satisfying about a shift like this—steady, busy, with just enough chaos to keep things interesting.

I glance at the clock, realizing my shift is almost over. One more hour, and then I'm free. The thought of going home, maybe catching a quick nap before figuring out what comes next, is tempting. But there's also a part of me that doesn't want the day to end just yet.

"Sasha, you got another table," Jackson calls from the kitchen, snapping me out of my thoughts. "Table five's asking for you specifically."

I raise an eyebrow, my curiosity piqued, and make my way over to the table in question. It's a couple of college kids, bright-eyed and grinning, probably here on a study break or just looking to kill some time. They're mostly new faces, but they seem friendly enough.

"What can I get for you?" I ask, pulling out my notepad with a smile.

They place their orders—wings, extra spicy, with a side of fries—and I nod, jotting it down quickly. As I turn to leave, one of them calls out, "Hey, Sasha?"

I pause, looking back at them. "Yeah?"

The kid grins, a little sheepish. "Thanks for the recommendation on the hot sauce last time. You weren't kidding; it's the best we've had."

I laugh, nodding in acknowledgment. "Told you. Stick with me, and I'll make sure you eat right."

He gives me a thumbs-up, and I head back to the kitchen, my mood lifting a little higher. It's the little things like that—the small connections, the moments of shared laughter—that make this job more than just work. It's about people and making someone's day a little better, even if it's just with a plate of wings and a joke.

By the time my shift ends, I'm tired but content, my

pockets a little fuller and my heart a little lighter. I untie my apron, hang it back on the hook, and give Jackson a quick wave as I head for the door.

"See you Monday night, boss," I call over my shoulder.

"Take care, Sasha," he replies with a grin. "And don't stay out too late this time!"

I laugh, stepping out into the afternoon sunshine.

The streets are alive with the usual buzz of New Orleans —tourists weaving through the sidewalks, music spilling out of every open door, the scent of street food mingling with the thick, humid air. I tuck my hair tie into my bag, feeling a pleasant heaviness in my pocket from the tips I've earned today. It's been a good day, simple and steady, and my thoughts drift back to Evie, to the soft, quiet moments of the morning that still cling to me like a favorite song.

As I turn down a quieter street, I decide to finally check my phone. I'm not much of a phone person. Usually, it's just a tool for work schedules and the occasional text from Glass. I hadn't even given Evie my number yet, but I find myself hoping, just a little, that maybe she found a way to reach out. I dig my phone out of my bag and swipe it open, glancing at the screen as I walk.

There's a notification: a new message from an unknown number. My heart skips, a little burst of excitement sparking inside me. Maybe it's her. I open the message, and the words make me smile instantly.

Hey, is this Sasha?

It's got to be Evie. Who else could it be? The thought sends a warm rush through me, and I can't help but type back a quick, flirty reply, my fingers moving faster than my mind.

Hey, beautiful, you found me. I was just thinking about you! Just finished my shift at Bourbon Wings. What about you?

I hit send, already picturing Evie's smile when she reads it. But almost immediately, a new message comes through, and the words make my stomach drop.

Are you Sasha Bennett from Westchester?

My breath catches, and my heart starts to pound, the lightness of the moment evaporating in an instant. It's like a switch flips in my brain, and suddenly, all the warmth and ease I've been carrying with me turns to ice. I stare at the screen, the familiar, dreaded name of my past staring back at me, and every instinct I've trained myself to follow kicks in at once.

It's not Evie. It's someone else. Someone who knows too much; someone who's reaching into a part of my life I've spent years trying to bury.

Panic flares, hot and fast, twisting my thoughts into a tangled mess of fear and frustration. I don't know who this is, how they got my number, or what they want, but I can't risk finding out. I can't let my past crawl back into this new, fragile thing I'm trying to build. My fingers fumble over the screen, my chest tightening as I try to steady my breathing. Without hesitating, I block the number, the screen blinking back to my home page as if nothing happened.

But I can't shake the feeling. The moment is ruined, my sense of calm shattered by the sudden reminder of who I used to be—who I've been running from. I shove my phone back into my bag, my hands trembling as I pick up my pace, trying to put as much distance as I can between me and that message. The city around me feels sharper now, every sound too loud, every step too quick.

I thought I was past this. I thought I could keep the past buried. But now, all I can think about is how quickly everything can unravel, how one message can pull me right back to where I never wanted to be again.

I take a deep breath, trying to shake it off, to remind myself of everything that's good, everything that's new. Evie's face flashes in my mind—her smile, her laugh, the warmth of her touch—and I cling to that image like a lifeline. I won't let this ruin what I have now. I won't let the ghosts of my past pull me under.

I keep walking, my steps quick and determined, focusing on the path ahead, on the present, on everything I've built here. I have no intention of looking back.

11

EVIE

The bookstore feels alive today, buzzing with an energy that always fills me up when I step inside. It's a quiet hum, a kind of electricity that crackles in the air when I prepare for poetry night. As I flick on the lights, the warm glow spreads through the space, illuminating rows of books and the small stage in the corner. It isn't much—just a wooden platform with a mic stand—but it's the heart of this place, where voices find their wings.

I start rearranging the chairs, each one holding its own story. Some are old, wobbly things my grandmother had picked up years ago at a yard sale; others are new and sturdy, but still feel like they belong. I line them up neatly, knowing that by the end of the night they'd be scattered and moved around in the happy chaos of people finding their place.

As I adjust the mic stand, the bell above the door jingles, and I turn to see Mrs. Landry sweeping in with her usual flair. She is a sight in a bright purple dress, a chunky necklace, and those gold bangles that clink with every step. Mrs. Landry has been coming here since before I was born, and her presence feels like a link to every past version of this bookstore.

"Morning, Evie!" she calls, her smile as big as ever. "Look at you, all busy and important. You getting ready for tonight?"

I laugh, giving her a quick hug. "Always. You know me, Mrs. Landry. I've got to make sure everything's just right. You coming tonight?"

She nods, her eyes sparkling. "Wouldn't miss it for the world. I remember when your grandmother used to have these nights. They were packed to the brim with people spilling out onto the sidewalk. You've got the same touch, Evie. This place feels just as magical as it did back then."

I smile, feeling the warmth of her words settle in my chest. "Thanks. I'm just trying to keep the tradition going. She really knew how to make people feel at home."

"She'd be so proud of you," Mrs. Landry says, giving my arm a gentle squeeze. "You're doing something special here, you know that?"

I nod, my throat tightening with gratitude. Mrs. Landry wanders off to her usual corner of the store, flipping through the new arrivals, and I take a moment to soak in the familiarity of it all. This is what I love most about the bookstore—not just the books, but the people who fill it, each of them bringing their own stories, their own energy.

I go back to setting up the event, making sure the chairs are spaced just right and the stage looks welcoming. As I straighten the last row, the door jingles again, and I look up to see Malik, one of my regulars, slipping in with his ever-present notebook clutched to his chest.

"Hey, Malik," I call, waving him over. "You ready for tonight?"

He shuffles his feet, giving me a shy smile. Malik is one

of those poets whose words burned brighter than he ever let on. Quiet and unassuming, but once he is on that stage, it's like watching a match strike in the dark.

"Yeah, I think so," he mumbles, glancing around nervously. "I've got something new, but...I don't know. It's different. I'm not sure if people will get it."

I hand him a stack of chairs to set up, knowing that keeping his hands busy would help settle his nerves. "Malik, people love hearing you read. It doesn't have to be perfect; it just has to be yours. That's what makes it special."

He nods, still looking unsure, but I see the flicker of a smile. "Thanks, Evie. You always know what to say."

As he moves off to set up the chairs, I feel a little burst of pride. Watching Malik grow as a poet, seeing him find his voice in this space, is one of my favorite parts of these nights.

I keep moving, arranging books on display and setting up the refreshments table with coffee, tea, and a few bottles of wine tucked discreetly at the back. I can already picture the room filled with people, the low murmur of conversations, the nervous excitement of those waiting to perform. I want tonight to feel special, and I can't help but hope that Sasha might walk through the door, bringing that spark she always seemed to carry with her.

Lost in my thoughts, I don't hear the door open again until I look up and see Mr. Dupree, a local musician, striding in with his guitar slung over his shoulder. He's a regular fixture at these events, always ready with a new song or a story that can make the whole room laugh.

"Evie!" he calls, setting his guitar case on the counter. "What's the word? We all set for tonight?"

"Hey, Mr. Dupree. Just about. I'm glad you're playing. I heard you've got something new."

He grins like a kid with a secret. "I've been working on something a little different. Thought I'd shake things up. You think I should go with a love song or keep it upbeat?"

I lean against the counter, pretending to think it over. "You know, I think we've had enough love songs lately. Give us something with a beat, make people want to move."

Mr. Dupree laughs, strumming a few chords on his guitar. "Your grandmother always said the same thing. 'Make them dance, Mr. Dupree. Make them feel alive.' That woman knew how to throw a party."

I nod, a pang of longing tugging at my heart. "She really did. I'm just trying to keep the tradition alive, you know?"

"You're doing a damn fine job of it," he says, giving me a warm smile. "And hey, save me a dance tonight, alright?"

"Always," I promise, watching him head to his usual spot by the stage.

For a moment, I let myself drift back, thinking of the nights when my grandmother was at the helm, directing everyone with her infectious energy. She'd always been larger than life, someone who could light up a room just by walking into it. When she passed, I'd felt the weight of the bookstore shift onto my shoulders, heavy with the responsibility of keeping it all going. But days like this made it all worth it.

As I move through the store, I find myself lingering by the poetry section, running my fingers along the spines of books that hold memories I can never quite put into words. It's here in these aisles that my grandmother had taught me about the power of stories, the way a single line of poetry could cut straight to the heart.

But as much as this place is tied to my grandmother, there are also memories of my mother woven into the shelves. My mom was a wild spirit, never content to stay in one place. She'd drifted in and out of my life like a wayward breeze, always chasing something beyond my reach. I remember the few times she'd swept into the bookstore, full of grand ideas and big promises, only to disappear again before the ink on those promises was dry.

Her death had been sudden, jarring in its finality. I'd been just a teenager, trying to navigate the messy reality of losing someone who had never really been there in the first place. It was my grandmother who'd stepped up, filling the gaps my mom had left behind, teaching me to love the bookstore, to find solace in the rhythm of the community she'd built.

"Evie?" Kenneth's voice breaks through my thoughts, and I turn to see him standing with a box of new books, watching me with his usual gentle concern. "You okay?"

I blink, pulling myself back to the present. "Yeah, sorry. Just thinking about everything, I guess."

He sets the box down and leans against the counter. "This place means a lot to you and to everyone who comes through that door. It's a big thing, what you're doing."

I nod, feeling the weight of his words settle around me. "Sometimes it feels like I'm just holding on, you know? Like I'm trying to keep all the pieces together."

Kenneth smiles, the kind that reaches his eyes. "You're doing more than that. You're building something. And you're damn good at it."

I smile back, grateful for his steady presence. Kenneth is more than just an employee; he's a friend, someone who understands the unspoken layers of this place.

As the day wears on, the bookstore transforms piece by piece, taking on the look and feel of a space ready for something magical. I finish arranging the last few chairs and step back, taking it all in. The room is ready, waiting to be filled with voices and stories, with laughter and nerves and the kind of moments that kept me coming back, night after night.

I wander to the counter and pick up one of my grandmother's old poetry books, thumbing through the pages. I find a passage I love, one she used to read to me when I was young, and I let the words wash over me, grounding me in the memory of her voice.

The bell above the door chimes again, and I look up, half-hoping it might be Sasha. But it's just the wind this time, a gentle reminder that not everything comes when you want it to. I tuck the book under my arm and glance around the empty bookstore, feeling the quiet anticipation that fills the space. It's a different kind of stillness, one that isn't empty but expectant, like the bookstore itself is holding its breath, waiting for the night to begin.

I find myself standing by the front door, watching the sun dip lower outside, casting long shadows across the street. In just a few hours, this place will be full again, buzzing with life and voices echoing off the walls. And though I love the noise, people, and stories they bring, it's these quiet moments I cherish most. The calm before the crowd, the stillness before the first poem is read.

I turn my attention back to the poetry book in my hands, tracing the faded gold lettering on the cover. It was my grandmother's favorite, a collection of poems about love, loss, and the unbreakable ties of family. She used to read from it at every open mic night, her voice strong and clear, filling the room with a warmth that never failed to make people feel seen.

I miss her terribly at times like this, miss the way she could make everything seem so effortless. I miss my mother, too, in a different way—miss the idea of what we could have been. But standing here, in the place that has been my sanctuary and my inheritance, I feel their presence woven into every corner of this bookstore.

I put the book back on the shelf behind the counter and take a deep breath, letting the familiar smells of paper and ink settle my nerves. Tonight will be like every other night—different faces, new poems, the same electric energy that makes this place come alive. And yet, it will also be new, filled with possibilities I can't quite see yet.

My wanders to Sasha, of her laughter that morning, of the way she fit so naturally into the bookstore, like she'd always belonged. I find myself hoping she'll show up tonight, that she'll walk through the door and take her place among the other voices. I want her to be a part of this, to see what makes this place so special, to understand why it matters so much to me.

As the sun dips lower and the light outside turns soft and golden, I close my eyes and let myself imagine it—Sasha in the audience, a smile tugging at her lips as she listens to the words of strangers, finding her own place in the rhythm of the night.

∼

The bookstore is ready. The chairs are set, the lights dim just enough to make the space feel cozy, and the refreshments are laid out on the table. It's Saturday night, the biggest night of the week, the night when the bookstore truly comes alive.

Saturday nights have always been special. They are different from the quieter midweek events—bigger, louder, with a little more energy in the air. People don't just come to read or listen; they come to connect, to let loose a bit, to

The Words of Us 107

celebrate the week's end with poetry, music, and each other. It's a night of possibility and new beginnings, and I always feel a certain thrill in the air as the hour approaches.

There's a tradition I've kept going since my grandmother's time: opening the night with a poem. It's my way of setting the tone and inviting everyone into the space, and it's something I look forward to each week. But tonight, the choice feels more important, more significant somehow. Maybe it's because of the memories that have surfaced throughout the day or the hope that Sasha might walk through the door. Whatever it is, I want to choose something that captures the spirit of the night—the joy, the energy, and the subtle undercurrent of something new, something exciting.

I move through the shelves, my fingers trailing over the spines of the books I know so well. My mind sifts through the possibilities, recalling lines and verses that have stayed with me over the years. I want something upbeat, something that will make people smile, but also something that hints at the spark of new love, at the thrill of connection that is so palpable in the air tonight.

As I scan the titles, a familiar name catches my eye: Langston Hughes. I pull the slim volume from the shelf and flip through the pages, pausing when I find the poem I'm looking for. It's perfect—light, rhythmic, and filled with that sense of hope and joy that I want to share with everyone here tonight.

The poem I chose is "Juke Box Love Song" by Langston Hughes. It has that easy, musical quality that fits a Saturday night, and the verses speak to the simple, pure joy of love, of being swept up in a moment with someone new. It's a poem that captures the essence of the night, the spirit of the bookstore, and the unspoken anticipation that hums beneath the surface.

I take the book with me to the small stage, placing it on the stand as people began to filter in. The familiar faces of regulars mix with newcomers, all of them settling into their seats with the casual ease that comes from knowing they are in a place where they belong. Mr. Dupree is already tuning his guitar, his fingers moving deftly over the strings, filling the space with soft, warm notes.

As I step up to the mic, the room quiets, the murmurs fading into an expectant hush. I look out at the faces in front of me, feeling a swell of affection for each and every one of them. These are my people, my community, and it's moments like this that makes every long day worth it.

"Good evening, everyone," I begin, my voice steady and warm. "Thank you all for being here tonight. As always, it's a pleasure to see so many familiar faces—and to welcome those of you who are new. Tonight's going to be special. I can feel it."

There's a ripple of agreement and a few soft laughs, and I smile, letting the energy of the room lift me up. "To start us off, I'd like to share a poem that's always felt like a celebration to me. It's about love, music, and the simple joy of being with someone who makes your heart dance. This is 'Juke Box Love Song' by Langston Hughes."

I open the book, the familiar words flowing through me as I begin to read:

"I could take the Harlem night
and wrap around you,
Take the neon lights and make a crown,
Take the Lenox Avenue busses,
Taxis, subways,
And for your love song tone their rumble down.

I could take the Harlem night
and wrap it round you,
Take the neon lights and make a crown."

The words hang in the air, filling the space with their rhythm, their music. I feel the connection in the room deepen, a shared appreciation for the simple beauty of the poem, for the way it captures that feeling of new love, of excitement, of something just beginning.

As I finish, there is a soft, appreciative murmur from the crowd, and I close the book with a contented smile. The night has begun, and with it, the promise of something more—more stories, more voices, more moments of connection.

But then my eyes drift to the back of the room, where the shelves are a little more organized than they'd been this morning. I don't even notice the door open, don't hear the bell's soft chime in the midst of my reading. But there she is, leaning casually against the very shelves where we'd tangled ourselves up the night before, where books had fallen around us like confetti.

Sasha.

She watches me with a look that's a half-smile, half something deeper—something that makes my heart skip and my breath catch. She stands there, almost like she's meant to be part of the bookstore's rhythm, fitting seamlessly into the scene. She is so effortlessly attractive, I almost can't bear it. Her eyes meet mine, and in that instant, the noise of the crowd fades, and it feels like it's just the two of us, connected by the invisible thread of last night and whatever is building between us.

The moment hangs there, suspended in the soft light, as she gives me that crooked, teasing smile I've come to love.

It's the kind of smile that says a thousand things at once—*I'm here. I'm with you. Let's see where this goes.*

I can't help but smile back, the unexpected thrill of seeing her standing there, in this place that meant everything to me, sending a rush of warmth through my veins. It's a small, quiet moment in a room full of people, but to me, it feels like the start of something big, something that can grow into whatever we are brave enough to let it be.

As I step off the stage and the next performer takes their place, Sasha stays by the shelves, her gaze never leaving mine. I make my way through the crowd, weaving between the chairs, laughter, and buzz of conversation rising around us. When I reach her, she leans in, her hand reaches for my cheek and I feel the cool touch of her fingers, her voice stays low, just for me.

"That was beautiful." Her words are like a soft note against the music still playing in the background. "But I think you already knew that."

I laugh, feeling that familiar, easy connection between us. "I'm glad you're here."

Sasha's smile widens, her eyes sparkling with mischief and something gentler. "I wouldn't miss it."

Her hand casually drops, lingering just a second as the pad of her index finger flicks over my lips.

And just like that, the night feels a little brighter and the bookstore a little warmer with her standing beside me.

12

SASHA

I hadn't planned on reading tonight. In fact, as I walk into the bookstore, all I want is to slip into the comforting anonymity of the crowd, to blend into the buzzing atmosphere of Saturday night poetry at Evie's. I've spent the day trying to shake off the tension of that unexpected message on my phone, telling myself over and over that the past can't touch me here. And when I see Evie up on stage, reading that poem, the way her voice carries softly through the room, I know I made the right choice to come.

The bookstore is more alive than I've ever seen it. Chairs fill up quickly, the low hum of conversation mixing with the strumming of Mr. Dupree's guitar. Wine flows, laughter bubbles up, and there is this infectious energy in the air that makes everything feel just a little bit brighter. It's the kind of night that makes me think anything is possible, and Evie is at the center of it all, orchestrating the magic like she was born to do it.

I linger by the back shelves, watching as the night unfolds. Performers come and go, each leaving a little piece of themselves on the stage. There was a young woman with a trembling voice who read about first loves and heartbreaks; an older man with a booming laugh who spun stories like they were old jazz records; and Malik, who stood at the mic with his head down but his words sharp and clear, cutting through the noise with a quiet confidence that I admire.

I should be happy just to watch, to take it all in from the safety of my corner. But as the night goes on, I can't shake the restless feeling in my chest. My fingers keep finding their way to the crumpled notebook in my bag, tracing the edges of the pages where I'd scrawled bits and pieces of a poem earlier in the week. It isn't finished—not even close—but it feels urgent, like something I need to say, even if I'm not sure who I'm saying it to.

I glance at Evie, who is leaning against the counter, smiling at something Kenneth has said. She looks so at home, so effortlessly part of this place, and when her eyes meet mine, I feel a jolt of something I can't quite name. It's like she can see right through me, past all the walls I've built, and in that moment, I want nothing more than to be part of her world, to step out of the shadows and into the light she seems to radiate.

Before I can talk myself out of it, my feet move toward the stage. My heart is hammering, my palms suddenly slick with nerves, but there is no turning back now. The next reader has just finished, and the mic is open, waiting for the next voice. My voice.

I hesitate at the edge of the stage, feeling the weight of every eye in the room on me. I don't do this often—not like this, not without preparation. But something about tonight, about this place and these people, make me feel like maybe I can. Maybe I need to.

Evie catches my eye again, and she gives me a small, encouraging nod. It's all the push I need.

I step up to the mic, my throat tight and dry, and adjust it to my height. The room falls quiet, a silence that's both terrifying and exhilarating. I glance down at my notebook, the messy handwriting staring back at me, and take a deep breath.

"Uh, hey," I begin, my voice cracking slightly. "I wasn't planning to read tonight, but...I don't know. There's something about this place that just pulls you in, right? So, I figured I'd share something I've been working on. It's, well, it's still rough, but it's real, and I guess that's what matters."

I can see Evie from the corner of my eye, her expression warm and attentive, and it gives me the courage to start. I look down at the page, and as I begin to read, the words feel less like mine and more like something that has been waiting to be spoken.

"We speak in whispers, soft and slow,
Afraid of things we don't yet know.
In glances shared and words unsaid,
We tiptoe toward what lies ahead.
A spark, a smile, a fleeting touch,
A promise that we want too much.
We build our bridges, one by one,
Afraid to fall, but drawn to run.
The walls we keep are thin as air,
A fragile shield we always wear.
But here, tonight, with you so near,
I find it's worth the risk to care.
We write the stories on our skin,
The places where the light gets in.
And though the end's a mystery,
I'm here for all that's yet to be."

As the last words leave my lips, I let out a breath. The silence that follows is thick, not with judgment, but with something else—an understanding, a connection that I don't expect. I glance up, and the room is still, every face turned toward me, every eye holding a glimmer of something that makes my heart swell.

I haven't realized how much I need this. The release of it, the feeling of being heard, of letting the walls come down just a little. There is a moment of quiet, then the room erupts in applause, warm and genuine, washing over me like a wave. I feel the weight of it, the affirmation that my voice matters here, that I'm not alone in whatever I'm feeling.

As I step down from the stage, my legs a little shaky, I make my way back toward the shelves, the adrenaline still buzzing in my veins. I am overwhelmed, but in the best way, caught between the rush of the performance and the realization that this place, this night, is becoming something more to me.

The room feels suddenly too full, too charged, and I slip out the back door to get air, the cool night air hitting me like a splash of water. I lean against the brick wall, closing my eyes and letting the quiet settle around me. My heart is still racing, but there is a sense of calm beneath it, a kind of peace I haven't felt in a long time.

The door opens softly, and I look up to see Evie step out, her expression a mix of pride and something softer, something that makes my stomach flip. She doesn't say anything at first, just moves to stand beside me, her shoulder brushing mine as she leans against the wall.

"You were amazing," she says finally, her voice low and sincere. "I'm so glad you read."

I shrug, trying to play it off, but the compliment warms

me in a way I'm not prepared for. "Thanks. I wasn't sure... I mean, it's been a while since I've done anything like that, reading without being prepared. But this place, it just makes you want to, you know?"

Evie nods, her eyes fixed on the street beyond. "I get it. That's why I keep doing these nights. It's like the room gives you permission to be exactly who you are. No judgment, no pressure, just space to be real."

I glance at her, catching the hint of vulnerability in her words. She's built this place, this haven, not just for others, but for herself too. It's part of her, just like the poems she reads, the way she moves through the crowd, the smile she gives to every performer who stepped up to the mic. I feel a surge of admiration for her, mixed with the thrill of knowing I am becoming part of this world she's created.

"I almost didn't come tonight," I admit, the confession slipping out before I can stop it. "I got this weird message earlier, and it just...rattled me, I guess. Made me want to hide."

Evie looks at me, her gaze steady and reassuring. "I'm glad you didn't. I'm glad you're here."

I feel a smile tug at my lips, small but genuine. "Me too. And hey, your poem, it was perfect. I could listen to you read all day."

She laughs softly, the sound like music in the quiet alley. "You might be the only one who thinks that."

"Not a chance," I say, turning to face her fully. "You have this way of making everything feel lighter. I don't know how to explain it. Like being around you makes things better."

Evie's cheeks flush, and for a moment, she looks almost shy. "That's really nice to hear. I've been thinking a lot today about why I do this, why I keep this place going. And it's because of moments like this. People like you."

We stand there, the night wrapping around us like a warm blanket, the distant sounds of the bookstore filtering through the door. There is so much I want to say, but I don't know how to put it into words. All I know is that I want more of this—more nights like tonight, more moments with Evie, more of the feeling that has been building since the moment I walked into the bookstore that first time.

"So, what's next?" Evie asks, her voice soft and tentative, like she's testing the waters of whatever is happening between us.

I think about it, about the uncertainty of the future, the weight of the past, and the possibility of something new. I reach for her hand, linking my fingers with hers, and give it a gentle squeeze.

"I don't know," I say honestly. "But I'm here for it. Whatever it is."

Evie smiles, her eyes bright with unspoken promise. "Yeah. Me too."

And as we stand there under the soft glow of the streetlights with the bookstore's muffled sounds of poetry and music behind us, I know that this is where I'm supposed to be.

The air between us feels charged, heavy with unspoken words and the quiet rhythm of our breaths mingling in the cool night. Evie's hand is still in mine, warm and reassuring, grounding me in the moment. The way her fingers tightens slightly around mine sends a spark of something hot and electric through me, something I've been trying to ignore but can no longer deny.

Her eyes search mine, full of something deep and unguarded that makes my heart beat faster. There's a softness there, a quiet intensity that pulls me in. For a moment, neither of us speak, the space between us thick with anticipation, with the weight of everything unsaid.

Evie takes a small step closer, the movement slow, deliberate, like she is giving me every chance to pull away. But I don't. I can't. I am rooted to the spot, caught in the pull of her presence, the nearness of her. The soft glow of the streetlights play over her features, casting delicate shadows on her skin, and I am suddenly overwhelmed by how close she is, by the quiet, intimate moment we've found ourselves in.

Her free hand lifts, brushing a stray lock of hair away from my face, and I feel a shiver run through me at the lightness of her touch. She lingers there, her fingers tracing the line of my jaw, her thumb brushing the corner of my mouth in a gesture so tender it makes my breath hitch.

"I've been wanting to do this all night," she murmurs, her voice barely more than a whisper, thick with the vulnerability of the moment. Evie's eyes flickers with something raw and unguarded, and in that heartbeat, she moves closer, her lips brushing mine in the gentlest, softest kiss. It's tentative at first, a careful exploration, as if she is feeling out the edges of something fragile. Her lips are warm and soft, and she tastes faintly of the wine we've been drinking, sweet and a little bold.

The kiss deepens slowly, and I feel everything else slip away—the noise from the bookstore, the hum of the city beyond, even the lingering doubts that has haunted me earlier. All that matters is this—the slow, deliberate press of her lips against mine, the way she moves with a careful, deliberate hunger that sends warmth pooling in my chest.

Evie's hand slides up, cupping the back of my neck, her fingers threading through my hair as she pulls me closer. I sink into her touch, my own hands finding their way to her waist, feeling the soft curve of her body beneath my palms. The kiss is unhurried, like we have all the time in the world, and every brush of her lips feels like a promise, a silent affirmation that this is real, that we are real.

I can feel the smile ghosting on her lips as she kisses me, a playful tease that makes my stomach flutter. She pulls back just a fraction, her forehead resting against mine, her breath mingling with my own in the small, shared space between us. My heart races and my skin tingles from the warmth of her touch, and for a moment, I just close my eyes, letting myself be held in the quiet.

Evie's thumb traces a gentle line along my cheek, her touch tender and sure. I open my eyes, meeting her gaze, and see the soft glow of affection mixing with something deeper, something that makes my pulse quicken. She leans in again, her lips brushing against mine with a slow, deliberate intensity that makes my knees feel weak.

She kisses me like she's savoring every second, like she's pouring every unspoken word, every hesitant feeling into the moment. It is soft but insistent, a careful blend of need and restraint, and I melt into it, my hands pulling her closer, wanting more of her, of this. Each kiss feels like a promise, a slow unveiling of everything we are too scared to say aloud.

When she finally pulls back, her breath warm against my lips, she doesn't move far. Her lips linger near my ear, and I feel her words more than hear them, the soft, whispered promise that sends a shiver through me.

"Later, you're mine."

Her voice is low, tinged with a quiet possessiveness that makes my skin flush and my heart skip a beat. It's a promise wrapped in heat, a pledge of something more to come, and it fills me with a heady, giddy anticipation.

I can't help but smile, my forehead still pressed to hers,

the moment suspended between us like a secret. There is something intoxicating about the way she said it, the quiet certainty in her voice.

"Yeah," I whisper, my voice soft but sure. "Later."

We stay like that for a moment longer, wrapped up in the warmth of each other, the night holding us in a tender embrace with a whispered promise of more, and the quiet, undeniable truth that I am hers, just as much as she is mine.

13

EVIE

The last guest has left, and the bookstore is finally quiet, save for the soft, lingering notes of Mr. Dupree's guitar still hanging in the air. I lock the door behind me, the click of the latch sealing us in, wrapping Sasha and me in the intimate silence of the night. My heart is racing, a mix of nerves and excitement thrumming through me, fueled by a couple glasses of wine I've already had. Tonight feels different—charged with possibility—and I want to make the most of it.

I glance over at Sasha, who is standing near the shelves, running her fingers absently over the spines of books, lost in thought. How she looks in this space like she belongs here makes my breath catch. I want this night to be special, something more than just an ending to the poetry event. I want it to feel like a continuation of the last time we spent the night together in the bookstore.

I move to the small table near the stage where we'd talked earlier, where our fingers had brushed and lingered, where the unspoken tension between us had been almost palpable. The wine bottle is nearly empty, but there is just enough for two glasses. I pour it carefully, watching the dark red liquid swirl into the glass, catching the light from the dimmed lamps above.

I set the glasses down on the table, arranging them carefully, making sure everything feels just right. My hands are steady, but inside, I am buzzing with anticipation, every nerve on edge. I reach behind the counter, pulling out the old, woven blanket we curled under before. I spread it out on the floor, turning the space into a makeshift little haven.

I look around, taking in the way the soft light touches everything—the gentle glow of the books, the flicker of candlelight I'd set on the counter, the muted shadows that stretches across the room. It is intimate, cozy, exactly how I want it to feel. My fingers trace the edges of the blanket as I smooth it out, feeling the quiet weight of the moment. I reach for a stack of poetry books I'd pulled earlier—some of my favorites, filled with verses that speak of love and longing, hope and new beginnings. I want the night to feel light, easy, but also honest, like the kind of conversation you only have when you're two glasses deep and the rest of the world has faded away.

I set the books within reach, flipping one open to a page I love, the words dancing in my mind as I imagine reading them to Sasha. The poems are a mix—some playful and light, teasing in their rhythms; others more tender, touching on the quiet moments that make you feel seen. I hope they'll be enough to bridge the gap between us, to turn this night into something that isn't just about attraction, but connection.

As I step back to look at what I've created, I feel a flutter of nerves. It's simple, nothing extravagant—just wine, blankets, and poetry. But it's ours, and that makes it feel meaningful.I catch a glimpse of her, still near the shelves, and I call softly, "Hey, come here.".

Sasha turns, her eyes meeting mine, and there's something in her expression—curiosity, maybe, or something softer, more vulnerable—that makes my pulse quicken. She walks over, her movements unhurried, and as she gets closer, I feel the space between us shrink to nothing.

I gesture to the setup, trying to keep my smile casual, though my heart is hammering in my chest. "I thought maybe we could stay a little longer. Just us."

Sasha's gaze shifts to the blanket, the glasses of wine, and the stack of poetry books resting within easy reach. Her smile is warm, and it lights something inside me. She doesn't say anything at first, just taking it all in, and when she finally looks back at me, there's a quiet understanding in her eyes that makes me feel seen in a way I don't expect.

"This is perfect," she says, her voice soft and genuine, and it's all the reassurance I need.

I hand her one of the glasses, our fingers brushing against each other's, and we sit down together on the blanket, the night settling around us like a secret. The candles flicker as we sip our wine, and I feel the last of my nerves melt away.

We don't need to rush. The poems are there, waiting for when we are ready, but for now, it's enough just to be here and share this space. The attraction between us is still there, humming beneath the surface, but so is something deeper, something that feels like the start of a story I'm not sure how to tell just yet.

But I want to try.

We curl up on the blanket, our shoulders touching as we settle into the small, cozy space. The room feels like it's just ours now—quiet and intimate. Sasha's presence next to me is grounding yet electric, and the simple act of being close to her feels like something I want to savor.

I reach for the stack of poetry books, my fingers grazing over the covers until I find the one I'd marked earlier. It is an old collection—well-loved, the pages worn and softened over time. I flip it open to the poem I've been thinking about all night, the one that feels right for this moment, with its sensual, lingering lines that speak of touch and connection.

"This one's always been a favorite of mine," I say, my voice hushed, the words barely above a whisper.

Sasha looks at me, her eyes dark and curious, and I feel my heart stutter at the way she watches me. I clear my throat, settling the book in my lap, and begin to read, my voice slow and deliberate, each word hanging in the air between us.

We linger in shadows, close and near,
With whispered secrets, soft and clear.
Your breath on my skin, a gentle trace,
The slow, sweet burn of this hidden place.
We speak in touches, fingers glide,
Mapping the curves we've yet to hide.
Your lips, a promise, warm and true,
A taste of wine, of me and you.
The night is ours, no rush, no fear,
With every kiss, you pull me near.
A dance of fire, slow and kind,
Our bodies sway, our hearts entwined."

My voice is steady, but each word feels like an intimate confession, exposing a part of me I haven't dared to share until now. I can feel Sasha's gaze on me, the way her eyes linger on my lips as I read, and it makes my pulse quicken, my skin warm under the heat of her attention.

When I finish, the silence between us is thick, charged

with the weight of the poem's sensuality, the quiet promise of something more. Sasha's lips parts, as if she is about to say something, but instead, she sets her glass down and moves closer, her movements slow, unhurried, like she's savoring every second.

She doesn't say a word. She just looks at me, her eyes soft and intent, and I can feel the pull, the magnetic draw of her that has been there from the start. I set the book aside, the pages falling shut, and turn to her, our faces inches apart. I can smell the wine on her breath, rich and heady, mingling with the faint scent of her perfume.

Sasha's fingers brush the side of my cheek, a light, teasing touch that sends a shiver through me. She leans in, her lips hovering just above mine, and for a moment, we just stay there, the anticipation buzzing between us. I can feel her breath, warm and steady, the closeness of her making my heart pound.

Then she closes the distance, her lips meeting mine in a soft, lingering kiss. It is gentle at first, tentative, as if testing the waters, but it quickly deepens, fueled by the wine and the quiet intensity of the moment. Her mouth is warm and sweet, tasting of the dark, earthy notes of the wine, and I find myself sinking into it, my own lips parting to meet her.

I kiss her back, slowly at first, savoring the way she feels —soft, inviting, every movement a careful exploration. There is no rush, no urgency, just the slow, deliberate pace of two people finding each other in the stillness. I can taste the wine on her tongue, the mix of alcohol and something uniquely her, and it's intoxicating, heady in a way that makes me forget everything else.

Sasha's hand slides into my hair, her fingers curling at the nape of my neck, pulling me closer as the kiss deepens. I can feel the heat of her skin, the way her body presses against mine, and it sends a jolt of desire straight through me. I let myself melt into her, my hands finding their way to her waist, feeling the soft curve of her beneath my touch.

The kiss grows hungrier, more insistent, and I lose myself in it, in the warmth of her lips, the taste of wine, the soft sounds of our breaths mingling in the quiet bookstore. It feels endless like time has slipped away and there's nothing left but this—just us, tangled in the moment.

When we finally pull back, breathless and flushed, Sasha's forehead rests against mine, her eyes still closed, a smile ghosting on her lips. I can feel the steady thump of her heartbeat, the quiet affirmation that this is real, that we are here, together.

I cup her cheek, my thumb brushing lightly against her skin, and I lean in, my voice barely a whisper, thick with promise and the lingering heat of our kiss and I am brave- I say again what I said earlier. "Later, you're mine."

"Later is now," she whispers softly, her voice tinged with both challenge and invitation. The words send a spark of heat straight through me, igniting every nerve with a sudden, urgent need. There is no more room for hesitation, no space left between us for anything but action, desire pulling us closer, pushing us over the edge we've been teetering on all night. Sasha's lips crash into mine, the softness from before replaced by something fiercer, hungrier. The kiss is intense, desperate, as if we are trying to make up for all the moments we hold back, all the things we haven't yet said. Her hands are on me instantly, fingers tangling in my hair, pulling me closer as if she can't bear to have even an inch between us.

I can feel the heat of her, the way her body presses urgently against mine, and I match her intensity, my own hands roaming over her, finding the hem of her shirt and tugging it up with frantic, impatient fingers. We break apart just long enough for me to pull the fabric over her head, our breaths mingling in gasps, the cool air of the bookstore barely registering against the fire sparking between us.

My mouth finds hers again, and she kisses me back just as hard, just as needy, her teeth grazing my lower lip, sending jolts of pleasure and pain mingling together. There is nothing gentle about it now; this is raw, messy, and completely consuming. Sasha's hands are on my waist, pulling me closer, her touch hot and insistent as she slips beneath my sweater, fingers tracing the bare skin underneath.

I shiver at the contact, every nerve alive with anticipation, and I press against her, needing more, needing all of her. My hands fumble at the buttons of her jeans, the urgency between us palpable, like we are both afraid this moment might slip away if we don't grab hold of it now. Sasha's breath hitch as I push the fabric down, and I feel her fingers working at my own clothes, pulling at my waistband with the same desperate need.

We tumble onto the blanket, our bodies tangled in a mess of limbs and breathless gasps, the softness of the fabric beneath us barely registering as we reach for each other. Sasha's kisses are relentless, her lips finding my neck, my collarbone, leaving a trail of heat in their wake. Her touch is everywhere, demanding and sure, and I am lost in it, lost in the way she makes me feel seen and wanted and wild all at once.

"God, Evie," she murmurs against my skin, her voice ragged, filled with a mix of desire and something deeper. "I need you."

The words are a plea, raw and vulnerable, and they send my heart racing. I hook my leg around hers, pulling her closer, feeling the firm press of her body against mine. My hands explore her, sliding over the curves of her hips, her waist, memorizing every inch like I'll never get the chance again.

I push her back gently, just enough to meet her gaze, her eyes dark and filled with the same need that's coursing through me. There's no time for shyness, no room for second-guessing. I let my fingers trace the line of her jaw, then her lips, and I kiss her again, deeper this time, tasting the urgency on her tongue, the faint sweetness of the wine still lingering between us.

She responds instantly, her hands finding the clasp of my bra, fumbling slightly in her haste but not stopping or slowing down. I arch into her touch, the cool air meeting my bare skin as the fabric falls away, and the sensation sends a shiver of pleasure coursing through me. Sasha's mouth is on me again, lips and tongue exploring, discovering, and I can barely keep up, my own hands roaming over her in a frantic attempt to give back every bit of the need she's pouring into me.

Quickly, our clothes discarded carelessly around us. There is no thought, no hesitation—just the relentless drive to be closer, to feel skin against skin, to lose ourselves in this moment that feels inevitable.

We move together, every kiss, every touch frantic and feverish, fueled by the shared urgency that seems to consume us both. I can feel the rough edges of the books around us, the faint scratch of the blanket beneath, but none of it matters. All that matters is Sasha—the taste of her, the feel of her, the way she pulls me in and doesn't let go.

Our kisses grow messier, more desperate, hands grasping, pulling, nails digging into skin as we give in completely to the pull between us. I can feel the tension building, the sweet, aching need that only intensifies with every touch, every breathless whisper. We are tangled together, a knot of desire and longing, and I don't care about anything else—not the past, not the future—only this, only now.

Sasha's lips find mine once more, and the kiss is so full of heat and hunger that it leaves me breathless and dizzy. Her hands grip my waist, pulling me closer until there is no space left between us, until every part of me is touching her, melting into her. We are a rush of heat and want, frantic and wild, and it's perfect, messy, unrestrained, and everything I haven't realized I've been craving.

As we move together, the world around us fades to nothing, and all I can feel is her on top of me—her thigh pushing my legs apart and pressing into my pussy.

I feel her right hand slipping down between us until her fingers are circling over my clit, sliding easily against me.

"Oh, Evie, you are so wet for me," she growls in my ear before taking my earlobe in her teeth. I feel her repositioning herself- I think so she can take her own pleasure from grinding against my thigh. I feel her own slick wetness there. I feel her fingers pushing lower, pressing inside of me, opening me up for her and she begins to fuck me.

And fuck me, she does. In and out, increasing in tempo, fingertips pressing into my G spot. I hear my own moans tear through the air with the deep pleasure I'm feeling.

I feel her against my clitoris too. Is it her hipbone? The heel of her hand? I don't know and it doesn't matter.

It is overwhelming and consuming, and I give myself to it completely, feeling the tension coil tighter and tighter until it snaps, pulling me under in a rush of heat and sensation of my climax that leaves me gasping and clinging to her.

Seconds later, I feel her grinding hard against my thigh, taking her own pleasure from my body. Her orgasm tears through her with ferocity and she cries out, "Evie..."

My name on her lips as she comes is the sweetest sound before she collapses into me, hot and heavy and beautiful.

We stay like that, tangled together on the blanket, our breaths mingling, bodies warm and slick against each other. The bookstore is quiet around us, the only sound the soft, ragged breaths we share. Sasha's forehead rests against mine, her eyes closed, and I can feel her heartbeat, wild and erratic, matching my own.

14

SASHA

The days with Evie blur together in the best way, each one a small snapshot of something that feels like a story unfolding between us, a slow, quiet rhythm we are both finding our way into. I can't remember the last time I have been so caught up in someone—in their presence, their words, the way they laugh at the smallest things. And it isn't just the big moments; it is the ordinary ones too, the quiet spaces between our conversations where we just are, wrapped up in each other like it is the most natural thing in the world.

I spend every free minute I can with her. We slip into a routine that feels effortless, like we have been doing this for much longer than just a couple of weeks. Days pass in stolen afternoons and evenings that turn into nights, each one painting another stroke on the canvas of whatever we are building together. We wander the city, Evie's hand always finding mine as we walk down the old streets of New Orleans, the humid air thick with the scent of jasmine and the distant hum of music.

One night, we find ourselves on a ghost tour, the kind

that weaves through the narrow alleys and past the old, haunted buildings of the French Quarter. We are just two faces in a crowd of tourists, but it feels like our own little adventure, something uniquely ours. The guide tells stories of long-dead lovers and restless spirits, and every time he leans into the dramatic, Evie squeezes my hand, her eyes sparkling with mischief and a barely contained laugh.

"This one's my favorite," she whispers as we pause in front of an old, crumbling mansion. "Supposedly, the woman who lived here still roams the halls, searching for her lost lover. But the guide never tells you she was a poet too. She used to sit on her balcony and read her words to the night."

I look at her, bathed in the glow of the lanterns, and I can see why Evie loves this story. It is romantic and tragic, wrapped up in mystery. Just like the woman in the story, Evie is filled with her own quiet poetry, and I am beginning to understand the verses that make her who she is.

When the tour ends, we find a small café tucked away from the noise, and we sit at a corner table, sharing a slice of lemon pie and sipping coffee as the night lingers around us. There is a soft jazz band playing in the background, their music spilling out onto the street, and I watch the way Evie's eyes sparkle, reflecting the flickering candlelight between us. We don't need to talk much; our silences are comfortable, filled with shared looks and easy smiles. It feels like we are both content to just be, soaking up the moment as if it is all that matters.

∼

Other days, we stay in, wrapped up in the comfort of each other's apartments. One evening, Evie shows up at my door with takeout and a bottle of wine, and we spend the night sprawled on my couch, eating noodles straight from the carton and talking about everything and nothing. She reads to me from a new poetry book she has brought, her voice soft and melodic, each word wrapping around me like a gentle embrace.

I listen with my eyes closed, letting her words wash over me, the cadence of her voice soothing and familiar. There is something intoxicating about the way she speaks—how every sentence feels like a secret she is sharing only with me. She pauses sometimes, catching my eye, and there is this unspoken understanding, a kind of intimacy that doesn't need defining.

On quieter mornings, we meet at the bookstore before it opens, the city still waking up around us. I help her set up for the day, rearranging books and restocking the coffee station while she tinkers with the display tables, always finding new ways to make the space feel fresh and inviting. We drink coffee together, sitting on the counter like teenagers sneaking in before class, talking about the poetry night lineups or the oddball customers who have wandered in.

One morning, she pulls out a notebook from behind the counter, sliding it across the table with a shy smile. "I've been working on something," she says, her cheeks flushing slightly. "It's not much, but…I don't know. It's been a while since I've tried to write anything."

I take the notebook, flipping through the pages, and I can see her in every line, every carefully chosen word. Her handwriting is neat, precise, but the words themselves are messy and raw, filled with the kind of vulnerability that makes my chest tighten. It is like she has poured herself onto the page, and I can't help but feel honored to be let in, to see this part of her she usually keeps tucked away.

"These are beautiful," I say, my voice soft. "You have something, Evie. You always have."

She looks at me then, her eyes wide and sincere, and for a moment, I think she might cry. But instead, she just reaches across the table, her fingers brushing mine in a touch that feels like everything she can't quite say aloud. We don't need to fill the silence with words. The quiet is enough.

There are nights when we stay up too late, losing ourselves in conversation that twists and turns with the hours. One evening, we end up in the park, sprawled out on a blanket under the stars, sharing a bottle of whiskey that burns sweet and warm as it goes down. The city is quiet around us, just the occasional rumble of a streetcar in the distance, and we talk about the things we usually keep hidden—our fears, our pasts, the ways we have both tried to run from who we are.

Evie tells me about her mom, the one who is always gone, chasing something that never includes her. I watch her face, the way it tightens with the pain she rarely lets show, and I listen as she lets it all out, piece by piece. When she is done, I reach for her hand, squeezing it gently, letting her know without words that I am there, that I see her.

She squeezes back, her smile soft and a little sad. "Thanks for listening," she says, her voice barely above a whisper. "I've never really talked about it. Not like this."

I lean in, pressing a kiss to her temple, my lips lingering just a moment longer than necessary. "You don't have to say thank you," I murmur. "I'm here. That's enough."

One afternoon, I find myself alone in my apartment, the late sun streaming through the window, warm and golden. I slip into the bath, letting the hot water soothe the lingering ache in my muscles, and I close my eyes, sinking deeper into the quiet. My thoughts drift to Evie, to the way she smiled at me that morning, soft and unguarded, and I can't help but smile too.

Every time I think of her, it feels like a spark catching, something bright and hopeful lighting up inside me. I think of the way she touches me, her fingers gentle and knowing, like she understands exactly what I need even before I do. I think of her laugh, how it can fill a room, and how her presence makes everything feel lighter, easier.

We haven't said the words. Not yet. But they are there, in every glance, every touch, in the way she pulls me close when she thinks I am not looking, and in the way I find excuses to be near her, to catch the soft scent of her hair or feel the warmth of her breath against my skin. It is in the small things—the way she reaches for my hand without thinking, the way I catch myself staring at her when she isn't looking, and the way she smiles when our eyes meet, like she knows exactly what is running through my mind.

I run my fingers through the water, watching the ripples spread, and I wonder how long this can last. I don't want to think about the future, about the inevitable messiness of feelings that run this deep, this fast. All I want is to hold onto the moments we have, to keep collecting them like snapshots, little pieces of a love story that is writing itself without either of us having to say a word.

We spend our evenings in the bookstore, sometimes reading aloud, sometimes lost in our own thoughts, comfortable in the shared silence. One night, Evie finds an old record player in the back room, and she brings it out, setting it up with a grin that makes her look ten years younger. She puts on a scratchy old jazz record, the kind that crackles and pops, and we dance between the shelves, swaying to the slow, sultry rhythm, the music wrapping around us like a second skin.

Evie's arms are warm around my waist, her cheek resting against mine, and I can feel her smile against my skin. It is soft, content, and I know then that whatever this is, it is something neither of us has planned, but both of us are already too far gone to turn away from.

Every day we spend together is another page in a story I don't want to end. We don't need to say the words; they are there in every kiss, every shared look, every time we curl up on the couch and let the world fall away. It is unspoken but understood, the quiet language of two people finding something they hadn't realized they were looking for.

And in every stolen moment, every whispered confession, I can feel it growing between us—a love that doesn't need to be declared, only felt, and it is enough.

∽

Glass and I are tucked away in the corner of a cozy wine bar, the kind that feels like a secret you want to keep to yourself. It is a quiet spot, dimly lit, with old jazz playing softly in the background. The kind of place that invites long conversations and the slow, easy buzz of a good bottle of wine. The evening is unseasonably warm, the doors propped open to let in the faint hum of the city, and I am grateful for the breeze that keeps the space feeling open and alive.

Glass is mid-story, his voice animated as he recounts his latest poetry reading, complete with dramatic gestures that have the couple at the next table glancing over with amused smiles. He is in his element, spinning the mundane into something theatrical, and I can't help but laugh at the way he mimics the exaggerated swoon of one of his audience members. Glass is a born performer, but more than that, he is a born friend—the kind who makes you forget your worries just by being near him.

"And then," he says, his eyes sparkling with mischief, "this guy stands up, right? And I swear, Sasha, he's got tears in his eyes—actual tears! I'm thinking, 'Wow, Glass, you really nailed it tonight,' but then he just yells, 'That was the worst thing I've ever heard!' Can you believe it?"

I laugh, nearly choking on my wine. "No way! What did you do?"

Glass leans back, swirling his glass with the kind of dramatic flair only he can pull off. "Oh, you know me. I bowed. Gave him the full performance. I mean, if you're gonna bomb, bomb spectacularly, right?"

"Right," I agree, still giggling. "You gotta own it. Make it part of the show."

"That's what I said!" Glass exclaims, pointing at me like I've just confirmed some universal truth. "Besides, it's not real art unless you get at least one person passionately hating it. That's the true test."

I shake my head, grinning at him. "You're ridiculous, you know that?"

He shrugs, taking a sip of his wine with a self-satisfied smile. "It's why you love me."

It's easy with Glass. Always has been. We slip into conversation like we're picking up threads we've never really put down. He knows my moods, my quirks, the way I sometimes disappear into my head when things get too heavy. And tonight, everything feels light, buoyed by the easy rhythm of his voice and the warm flush of the wine.

"You and Evie seem good," Glass says, his tone shifting

to something softer, more sincere. "I've never seen you this, I don't know, settled? Happy?"

I pause, caught off guard by how much the simple observation makes my heart swell. "Yeah, I think we are. She's...she's something else. I don't know how to explain it, but it's like everything just fits."

Glass smiles, genuine and warm. "You deserve that, Sash. You deserve someone who sees you. All of you."

I nod, trying to keep my smile steady, but it's hard to hide how much those words mean to me. I've spent so long feeling like the pieces of my life were scattered, and now, with Evie, it's like they're slowly coming together. I take another sip of wine, letting the moment linger between us.

"So, what's next?" Glass asks, raising an eyebrow. "You gonna be one of those obnoxiously cute couples now? Matching sweaters and finishing each other's sentences?"

I roll my eyes, nudging him playfully with my elbow. "Please. You know me better than that. But...yeah, I think I could get used to this."

We lapse into a comfortable silence, and I lean back, soaking in the atmosphere of the bar, the soft murmur of conversations and the gentle clink of glasses. Everything feels calm, settled, and I'm about to ask Glass about his next reading when my phone buzzes on the table, the screen lighting up with a new message from an unknown number.

I hesitate, my stomach tightening with an unwelcome sense of déjà vu. It's not the same number as before, but the sight of it alone is enough to send a ripple of unease through me. I glance at Glass, who's still blissfully unaware as he's finishing the last of his wine with a contented sigh. I take a breath and pick up the phone, unlocking it with a swipe of my thumb.

"Sasha, you need to respond. This is urgent."

The words stare back at me, cold and demanding, the urgency in them sharp and unmistakable. My heart rate spikes, the easy warmth of the evening evaporating in an instant. I stare at the screen, my mind spinning with questions, fear clawing at the edges of my thoughts. I don't recognize the number, but the message feels like it's reaching right through me, dragging up everything I've been trying to bury.

"Sash? You good?" Glass's voice pulls me back, and I quickly lock the screen, forcing a smile I don't feel.

"Yeah, yeah, I'm fine," I lie, shoving my phone into my bag as if that'll keep the message from looming over me. "Just spam. You know how it is."

But Glass isn't buying it. He knows me too well and sees right through the forced casualness in my tone. "Spam, huh? You sure? You look like you've seen a ghost."

I swallow, the wine suddenly tasting bitter on my tongue. "Yeah, just...unexpected. It's nothing."

Glass eyes me for a moment, his expression shifting from playful to concerned. He reaches out, resting his hand on mine, the gesture grounding me in a way I desperately need. "You don't have to talk about it, but I'm here, okay? Whatever it is."

I nod, but my mind is already a million miles away, replaying the message over and over in my head. I try to focus on the here and now, on Glass's familiar face, the comfort of his presence, but the weight of the words on my phone feels like a noose tightening around my chest.

Glass tries to steer the conversation back to safer ground, talking about the latest drama with his poetry group, but it's hard to concentrate. I nod along, forcing out a laugh when it seems appropriate, but my mind keeps drifting back to the message, to the urgency in those few short words. I can feel myself slipping, the walls I've built around this new life starting to crack, and all I want is to claw my way back to the easy, carefree moment we were having just minutes ago.

"I think I'm just tired," I say eventually, cutting Glass off mid-sentence. "Maybe too much wine. It's been a long week."

Glass watches me, his eyes searching mine, and I can tell he wants to press, to dig deeper into whatever's suddenly shifted in me. But he holds back, giving me space, even as his worry lingers in the way he squeezes my hand before letting go.

"Alright," he says gently. "But if you need anything—"

"I know," I cut in, my voice tight. "I promise, I'm fine."

We pay the bill, and Glass walks me to the corner where we'll go our separate ways, the city buzzing around us like nothing's changed. He gives me a hug, holding on a little longer than usual, and I lean into it, grateful for the anchor he's always been.

"Don't be a stranger, okay?" he says, pulling back just enough to look me in the eye. "Whatever's going on, don't shut me out."

I nod, but my smile feels strained, stretched too thin over the mounting dread simmering inside me. "I won't. Thanks, Glass."

We say our goodbyes, and as he disappears into the crowd, I pull my phone from my bag, my fingers trembling slightly as I stare at the message again. There's a tight knot of fear in my chest, the kind that hasn't loosened since the last time an unknown number reached out from my past. I don't know who it is or what they want, but I can't shake the feeling that whatever it is, it's not good.

I take a deep breath, trying to shake off the chill that's

settled over me, but it lingers, like a shadow creeping at the edges of this life I've started to build. I turn and head in the opposite direction, my footsteps heavy, the night feeling colder and sharper than it did just moments ago.

It's supposed to be different now, I tell myself. *I have Evie. I have a fresh start.* But as I walk, the message burns in my pocket, a constant, nagging reminder that the past has a way of finding you, no matter how far you think you've run.

15

EVIE

I wake up feeling a lightness in my chest, the kind that's been there more and more lately. Today, I get to see Sasha, and the thought of it pulls me out of bed faster than my morning coffee ever could. I've missed her, even though it's only been a day since we last saw each other. It's funny how quickly she's become a part of my daily routine, like her presence is something I've been missing all along without knowing it.

We've made plans to meet at our usual spot, a little café with mismatched chairs and faded art on the walls. It's become our place, the kind of cozy, tucked-away corner of the city that feels like it's just for us. I'm early, of course—I always am when it comes to seeing her—and I spend the time sipping my coffee and replaying moments from the last two weeks in my head. The late nights reading together, the way she looks at me when she thinks I'm not paying attention, the feeling of her hand slipping into mine as we walk down the street.

When Sasha finally arrives, the familiar jingle of the doorbell signaling her entrance, I look up with a smile, ready for the usual spark that lights up whenever she's near. But something is different today. She hesitates at the doorway for a moment, her eyes scanning the room like she's looking for something she's lost. When our eyes meet, she smiles, but it's not the easy, carefree smile I'm used to. It's tight, a little forced, and there's a flicker of something in her eyes that I can't quite place.

"Hey," she says, sliding into the chair across from me. She leans in for a kiss, quick and fleeting, and I catch the faint scent of her perfume mixed with something heavier, maybe worry. "Sorry I'm late."

"You're not late," I say, brushing it off, but the words feel hollow. I reach across the table, my fingers grazing hers, but she pulls back almost instinctively, picking up her menu, even though she knows it by heart. The small distance between us feels suddenly vast.

We order breakfast, and I try to fill the silence with light conversation—telling her about a quirky customer who came into the bookstore yesterday, making jokes about how Kenneth nearly dropped an entire stack of books when a mouse scurried across the floor. Normally, this would make her laugh, that bright, melodic sound that never fails to lift my spirits. But today, Sasha just nods, her eyes unfocused, and I can tell she's not really listening.

"You okay?" I ask, my voice softer, tinged with a concern I can't quite hide. "You seem...distracted."

Sasha looks up, and for a second, there's a flash of something—fear? Guilt?—before she smooths it over with a practiced smile. "Yeah, I'm fine. Just a lot on my mind."

She doesn't elaborate, and I don't push. I want to ask, to dig deeper, but something holds me back. Maybe it's the slight edge in her tone, the way her fingers drum restlessly on the table, or how she keeps glancing at her phone like she's expecting bad news. I tell myself she's just tired, that maybe work is stressing her out, but deep down, I know it's more than that.

As the morning goes on, I keep trying to pull her back, to find the rhythm we've had since we started this thing, whatever it is. I suggest a walk, hoping the fresh air will help, and she agrees, but there's a heaviness in her steps that wasn't there before. We wander through the city, past the colorful balconies and iron gates of the French Quarter, the kind of scene that usually sparks a story or a joke between us. But today, Sasha is quiet, her responses clipped, as if she's somewhere else entirely.

I point out a street musician playing an old blues tune, hoping to catch her attention, to get even a flicker of the Sasha I know. She pauses and watches for a moment, but the light in her eyes is distant, like she's seeing something far away. When I try to slip my arm around her waist, she leans in but doesn't quite settle, like she's holding something back, wrapped up in thoughts she won't share.

We find a bench by the river, and I suggest we sit for a while. The breeze is warm, the sun glinting off the water in a way that makes everything seem softer, easier. But Sasha's shoulders are tense, her posture is stiff, and I can feel the disconnect between us growing with every second of silence. I try again, asking her about her week, about her plans, but her answers are short, mechanical. The closeness we've built feels like it's slipping through my fingers, and no matter how hard I try, I can't seem to pull it back.

"Sasha," I say finally, turning to face her fully, my voice gentle but firm. "I know something's going on. You don't have to talk about it if you don't want to, but I'm here, you know?"

She nods, her gaze fixed on the river, her fingers twisting

the hem of her shirt. "I know, Evie. I do. I just...I can't right now."

The words sting more than I want to admit, but I force a smile, nodding as if that's enough. I reach for her hand again, and this time she lets me hold it, her grip loose but there. I try to draw comfort from the contact, but it feels fragile, like a lifeline that's fraying at the edges. I want to tell her that she can trust me, that whatever it is, we'll get through it together, but I'm scared of pushing too hard, scared of saying the wrong thing and losing her.

We sit in silence, and I watch her out of the corner of my eye, trying to read the lines of tension in her face, the tightness in her jaw. It's like she's here, but not really, and I don't know how to reach her. The Sasha I've come to know—bright, playful, always with that spark of mischief in her eyes—feels just out of reach, replaced by someone distant, guarded, wrapped up in something I can't touch.

Eventually, we head back to my place, and I put on a record, hoping the music will break the strange spell that's settled between us. Sasha sits on the couch, her legs tucked up beneath her, and I curl up beside her, resting my head on her shoulder. She wraps an arm around me, and for a moment, I think maybe things are okay. But the silence stretches, and I feel the familiar Sasha slipping further away.

We spend the rest of the afternoon in a quiet that's not quite comfortable, not quite tense, but something in between. I read, pretending to be absorbed in the book, but my mind keeps drifting back to the way Sasha's thumb scrolls absently on her phone, the way she glances at it every few minutes like she's waiting for something she doesn't want to see.

I want to ask what's wrong. I want to tell her that she

doesn't have to carry whatever this is alone, but I'm afraid of pushing her away. So I sit there, feeling the weight of the unspoken between us, hoping that whatever's pulling her away will let go soon, that she'll come back to me.

As the day fades into evening, I watch her get up, her movements slow and deliberate, like she's dragging herself through the motions. She kisses me goodbye at the door, a quick, distracted press of our lips that leaves me feeling colder than I like to admit.

"See you tomorrow?" I ask, trying to keep my voice light.

"Yeah," she says, but there's a hesitation, a flicker of something that tells me she's not sure. She gives me one last tight smile before she turns away, and I'm left standing in the doorway, watching her walk down the street, feeling more alone than I have in a long time.

I close the door and lean against it, letting the quiet of the apartment settle around me. I don't know what's going on with Sasha, but the sudden distance between us leaves me feeling adrift, like I'm losing something I've only just begun to find. I want to be there for her, but I don't know how, and the uncertainty gnaws at me, twisting in my chest like a knot I can't untangle.

As I move around the apartment tidying up, I find one of the poetry books we've been reading together last week. I flip it open to a random page, scanning the lines that once felt so connected to us but now seem hollow, echoing the quiet between us that I don't know how to fill.

I tell myself it's just a bad day, that whatever's going on will pass, and she'll be back,, the light and carefree Sasha I've come to know. But as I lie in bed that night, the emptiness of the space beside me feels impossibly wide, and I can't help but wonder if whatever's pulling her away is stronger than anything I can offer.

I close my eyes, holding onto the hope that tomorrow will be different, that the distance will fade, and we'll find our way back to each other. But sleep doesn't come easy, and in the quiet dark, all I can do is wait, feeling helpless and a little lost, unsure of how to bridge the gap that's opened up between us.

∼

The morning air is cool as I make my way to Sasha's apartment, the city still waking up around me. I don't know why I decided to come over so early, but I couldn't bear the weight of yesterday hanging over us. I've spent the whole night replaying our time together: the distance in her eyes, the way she seemed so far away even when she was right beside me. I just want to make it better, to feel that closeness we've built slip back into place.

I stop in front of her door, nerves fluttering in my stomach. My hand hovers over the wood, and for a moment, I consider turning back, giving her the space she seems to need. But then the door opens suddenly, and Sasha is there, her hair messy from sleep, her eyes wide and surprised, but there's a softness in her expression that makes my breath catch.

"Evie," she says, her voice a mix of surprise and warmth. She's still in one of my old t-shirts, her bare legs pale against the dim light filtering in from the window. "I wasn't expecting you."

I smile, sheepish, feeling a little ridiculous for showing up unannounced. "I just...-I wanted to see you. I couldn't stop thinking about yesterday."

Sasha steps aside, her smile widening, and something in her eyes has shifted. She looks lighter, like the weight that had been pressing down on her has lifted, if only just a little. "Come in. I'm glad you're here."

I step inside, the familiar scent of coffee and lavender greeting me. Her apartment feels warm, lived-in, and I can see the traces of her morning routine—an open book on the couch, a half-finished cup of tea on the counter, a notepad with half-scribbled lines of poetry. She looks more like herself today, less guarded, and I let out a breath, feeling relieved.

Sasha leads me into the kitchen, her fingers brushing mine as we walk, and I can feel the shift between us, the unspoken acknowledgment that today is different. She turns to face me, leaning against the counter, and there's a softness in her smile that makes my chest ache in the best way.

"I'm sorry about yesterday," she says, her voice quiet but sincere. "I've just had a lot on my mind. But I'm better now. I promise."

I step closer, my hands finding her waist instinctively, and I can feel the steady rhythm of her breathing, the warmth of her body against mine. "You don't have to apologize," I say, my thumb tracing gentle circles on her hip. "I just...I hate seeing you like that. I want to help."

Sasha leans into me, her forehead resting against mine, and there's a tenderness in the way she touches me, her fingers trailing up my arms, slow and deliberate. "You do help, Evie. More than you know."

The distance that had felt so wide yesterday seems to shrink in an instant, and before I can think too much about it, I close the gap, my lips finding hers in a kiss that's gentle, testing. Sasha responds immediately, her hands sliding up to cup my face, pulling me closer. There's a neediness in the way we kiss, like we're both trying to make up for lost time, for the moments we let slip away.

The kiss deepens, and I let myself get lost in it, in the soft, insistent press of her lips, the way her fingers tangle in my hair, tugging me closer. I can taste the faint hint of her toothpaste, fresh and minty, mixed with something sweet and unmistakably her. The kitchen feels warmer, the space between us charged with a familiar, magnetic pull.

Sasha's breath hitches as I move my hands to her hips, pulling her closer, and she presses against me with a soft, breathless sound that makes my heart race. I lift her easily, my hands steadying her as I guide her onto the counter. She gasps, her legs instinctively wrapping around my waist, and I feel the firm press of her thighs against my sides, pulling me in.

I run my hands up her bare legs, feeling the soft, smooth skin beneath my palms, and I push the hem of her T Shirt higher, exposing more of her as I go. Sasha's eyes are dark, focused, and there's a hunger there that matches my own, a need that's been simmering just below the surface.

"Evie," she gasps, her voice edged with a mix of urgency and something softer, something vulnerable.

I kiss her again, deeper this time, letting my hands roam freely, exploring every inch of her that I can reach. I push my hands underneath her shirt feeling her bare skin against my fingers. I trace the curve of her waist, the soft dip of her stomach, and I can feel the way her muscles tense beneath my touch. She's warm and responsive, and I can't get enough, can't get close enough.

Sasha's fingers dig into my shoulders, and she pulls me closer, our bodies fitting together perfectly. I press kisses along her jaw and down her neck, tasting the faint salt of her skin, and she tilts her head back, giving me access as her breath comes in quick, shallow bursts.

I pull back and part her legs further with my hands. I

can see the damp patch of her desire on her cotton panties. I trail my fingers along the softness of her underwear, feeling the heat of her through the thin material. She shivers, her hips lifting on the kitchen counter, and I meet her gaze, pausing for just a second, searching for any hesitation.

But all I see is want, clear and undeniable, and it's all the encouragement I need. I push the fabric aside, my fingers brushing against her wanting pussy, and Sasha's head falls back, her lips parting in a soft, breathless moan that sends a surge of heat through me. I move against her, my touch firm and deliberate, and she responds instantly, her body arching, every movement a silent plea for more.

I lean down replacing my hand with my mouth. My left hand holds her panties to the side as my tongue eats her hungrily.

I can't get enough of the taste of her in my mouth.

It feels like no amount of Sasha will ever be enough. She feels wetter and wetter the more I lick.

Her hips push forward against me.

"I want you to come in my mouth," I look up and stop what I'm doing and meet her gaze.

There's something else I want to do, my right hand moves underneath her taking the slickness from her pussy and rubbing it against her anus.

"Is this ok?" I ask, my voice thick with want.

She nods, her green eyes glazed with lust and I press at her asshole with my finger.

As my finger slides slowly into her, I hear a deep earthy moan from her. Her eyes close and her hand reaches for the back of my head pulling my mouth back to her pussy.

Long slow strokes of my tongue match the long slow thrusts of my finger deep in her ass.

I feel her tighten and tense and her hand pulls my face

so tight to her I can't breathe. And then she comes with a ferocity I had never imagined, gushing on my tongue, filling my mouth with her pleasure.

I swallow and swallow desperate to take every drop of her orgasm.

As she relaxes and releases her grip on my head I take a deep breath and go back to long slow tender licks of her and she begins to shiver under my touch.

I pull away and watch how beautiful she is as she opens her eyes.

"That was... so incredible..." her voice is throaty and raw, as though she can barely speak.

I help her down from the kitchen side and suddenly she is in my arms and kissing me with a renewed hunger.

"Please.. Evie... I need to taste you."

She is quick to strip off my clothes, she is still wearing her baggy t shirt and soaking panties.

She drops to the floor pulling me down with her in between kisses.

"Please... sit on my face," she says as she lies back on the cool kitchen tiles taking my hand and guiding me atop of her until I'm straddling her face on my knees.

She is looking up at me and my pussy is so close to her mouth I can feel her hot breath against it.

"Look in my eyes the whole time," she says. Her left hand is still holding my hand, I can feel movement behind me and I think her right hand is buried in her own panties touching herself.

I look down at her, the intensity of meeting her gaze as I lower my pussy to her mouth overcomes me, but I don't look away.

Her green eyes are full of lust as they look up at me, unashamed as they take in my breasts on their way to my face. Her moan as my pussy hits her mouth is raw and passionate like an animal and she begins to lick me deeply pushing her tongue inside of me then giving me long licks, nibbles, sucks. She fucks me with her mouth as though it is the thing she enjoys most in the world, and I don't know, maybe it is. I know she is touching herself as we do this and the thought of it turns me on no end. I can still taste her come in my own mouth.

My eyes are locked on hers and our fingers interlocked as I relax into it and begin to rock against her mouth.

I grind down and seek my own pleasure from her tongue, her mouth, her chin. I find delicious pressure for my clitoris and I lose myself in the intensity of her flashing green eyes.

"I'm going to come," I murmur, I can feel it building deep inside me. "Come with me," I say and I sense the movements of her hand quicken. She is passive now in my orgasm, I'll take my own pleasure by grinding into her mouth.

I see her own pupils widen as I take one last deep thrust of my pussy into her mouth and my orgasm floods through me, wave after wave. I hear her cry out into my pussy as she comes, too.

And we are both coming, still looking in each others eyes as though nothing else matters in the world.

Her hand squeezes mine and I feel her short nails digging into my flesh.

And in the beautiful chaos of it all with this incredible woman who is full of secrets, I know this—whatever was hanging over us yesterday—is gone now, lost in the heat of this moment and in the way we fit together, perfectly and completely.

For now, it's enough.

16

SASHA

I slam the door to my apartment behind me when I get home from work, the noise echoing through the small space louder than I intended. I'm trembling and my hands are shaking as I drop my bag onto the floor, and the thud of it feels final, like a gavel falling at the end of some silent trial. My heart is still racing from the day, from the morning with Evie, and from the message that has been burning a hole in my mind ever since I read it. It's like a film stuck on repeat, every word etched into the backs of my eyelids.

"Sasha, we need to talk. You can't keep ignoring this."

I drag myself into the bathroom, the small, cluttered space that feels like the only corner of the world where I can truly be alone. I flip the light on and stare at my reflection in the mirror, gripping the edges of the sink so tightly my knuckles turn white. I look at myself—really look—and I barely recognize the person staring back. My hair is messier than usual, and there's a rawness in my eyes that I don't know how to hide. I look like someone caught between two lives, two versions of myself, and I don't know which one to hold onto.

There's a tightening in my chest, a knot that's been building for weeks now, and it feels like it's finally about to snap. I squeeze my eyes shut, trying to breathe through it, but all I can hear is that message replaying over and over, like it's clawing its way out of some dark place I thought I'd buried.

I think about Evie—about the way she looks at me like I'm something good, something whole. But right now, staring at my own reflection, I can't see what she sees. I see all the mistakes and all the things I've been running from. The weight of my past feels heavy, like it's pressing down on my shoulders, threatening to crush the fragile happiness I've found with her.

I've spent so long pretending it doesn't matter, that the things I've left behind are just ghosts, faded memories that can't touch me anymore. But they do touch me. They cling to me, shadowing every step, every decision. They were there yesterday when Evie looked at me with that quiet concern, the same look that made my stomach twist because I know I'm letting her down. I'm holding back. And I hate it.

I open my eyes, staring myself down, trying to find the version of me that Evie believes in. But all I see is someone scared, someone trapped like a wild animal. I've tried so hard to keep my past at arm's length, to keep it out of the life I'm building now, but it's here seeping through the cracks, and I don't know how to stop it. I don't know how to keep it from ruining everything.

"Get it together," I whisper, my voice trembling. "You can't keep doing this."

I press my palms against the cool porcelain, grounding myself, forcing the panic back down. My phone buzzes on the sink beside me, and my stomach drops. I don't want to look, but I know I have to. I can't keep running from this. Not anymore. I snatch it up, my fingers fumbling as I unlock the screen.

Another message. Another reminder that my past isn't finished with me.

"Sasha, this isn't going away. You need to face it."

The knot in my chest tightens, and I feel like I'm going to break apart right here. I want to scream, to throw my phone against the wall and watch it shatter. But I can't. Because that won't change anything. It won't make this go away. I know that now.

I sink down onto the edge of the tub, my back against the cool tile, and I let myself feel it—all the anger, fear, and exhaustion of carrying this weight alone. I think of Evie and how she's starting to slip through my fingers, how every day I pull away from her just a little bit more because I'm too scared to tell her the truth. The truth that I'm not as put together as she thinks, that I'm haunted by things I haven't told her, and I don't know how to let her in.

I look at the message again, the words blurring as tears sting at the corners of my eyes. I'm tired of being scared. Tired of letting this shadow hang over me, dictating how I live, how I love. I can't keep letting my past define my future. I can't keep letting it steal away the things I care about most.

My fingers hover over the keyboard, hesitant at first, but then I feel a surge of something—anger, defiance, maybe even a shred of hope. I start typing, each word coming faster, more sure, like I'm clawing my way out of a pit that's been holding me down for too long.

"Leave me alone. That person doesn't exist anymore. I don't want this. I'm done."

I hit send before I can second guess myself, the message

shooting off into the ether. It's not a solution, I know that. But it's a step. It's me fighting back, refusing to let the past keep pulling me under. I sit there staring at my phone, waiting for a response that doesn't come, and for the first time in what feels like forever, I feel something like control.

It's small, a flicker of strength, but it's mine. I push myself up, staring at my reflection one last time, and this time, I see someone fighting. I see someone who wants to be better, who wants to let Evie in, and who isn't going to let fear keep running the show.

I turn off the bathroom light, leaving the message—and the person I used to be—behind in the dark. And as I step outside the bathroom, the weight in my chest eases just a little, like I'm finally starting to take my life back, one small victory at a time.

∽

The kitchen at Bourbon Wings is stifling tonight, the heat from the fryers mixing with the constant clatter of dishes and the sharp smell of hot sauce and grease. But for once, I don't mind the chaos. I'm throwing myself into it, letting the rhythm of the shift pull me in and drown out the noise that's been clouding my head for days. The music is loud, the tables are packed, and the rush of orders keeps my hands busy and my mind too occupied to wander.

I feel lighter since sending that message yesterday. Stronger. No more messages have come through, and for the first time in a long time, I feel like maybe I've done enough to put all of it behind me. Gareth can't touch me now, not here, not in this life I've built for myself. I keep reminding myself of that every time a flicker of doubt tries to creep back in.

Evie's meeting me after my shift, and just the thought of seeing her makes the long hours go by faster. I picture her smile and the way her eyes light up when she sees me, and it makes everything feel brighter. Better. I'm looking forward to sliding into that easy comfort of her presence, to holding her close and letting the day fade away.

The restaurant is winding down, the once rowdy crowd thinning out to just a few stragglers nursing the last of their drinks. I wipe down the last table, exhaustion settling into my bones. I grab my stuff from the back, clock out, and push through the swinging doors into the night, the cool air hitting me like a balm.

I'm reaching for my phone to text Evie when I see him leaning against the wall just outside the entrance, his face half-hidden in the shadows. My heart stops. I know that silhouette, the slouch of his shoulders, the way he's staring at me like he's been waiting all night. Gareth.

Every ounce of strength I'd felt today evaporates in an instant, replaced by a cold, creeping dread. I haven't seen him in so long, and I thought I'd never have to again. My feet feel rooted to the ground, a jolt of fear freezing me in place, but I force myself to move, to keep my face steady, even though my heart is pounding so hard I think it might burst.

"What are you doing here?" I snap, my voice sharper than I intend, but I don't care. I don't want him here. Not now. Not ever.

Gareth steps forward, the dim streetlight catching his face, and I see the same smug, infuriating expression that used to haunt me every day. "We need to talk, Sasha."

"No, we don't," I say, my voice shaking with barely restrained anger. "I told you to leave me alone. You don't get to just show up like this."

He smirks, unaffected, and the familiar arrogance in his eyes makes my stomach turn. "You can't ignore me forever."

"I can, and I will," I hiss, glancing around, hoping no one's watching this mess unfold. "Just go. We're done. I have nothing to say to you."

The tension is thick, his presence a suffocating weight that I thought I'd shed months ago. I'm about to turn and walk away, anything to put distance between us, when I hear footsteps approaching, quick and sure. I look up, and there's Evie, her expression shifting from concern to something darker as she takes in the scene.

"Sasha, everything okay?" she asks, her voice steady, but there's a flicker of uncertainty in her eyes. She looks between Gareth and me, trying to piece together what's happening.

Gareth turns, sizing her up with a lazy, dismissive look, and it makes my skin crawl. "This doesn't concern you," he says flatly, as if she's nothing more than an inconvenience.

Evie doesn't flinch. She steps forward, positioning herself between us, her presence instantly comforting and strong. "She's asked you to leave," she says firmly, her eyes never wavering from his. "So why don't you do that?"

Gareth scoffs, crossing his arms. "And who the hell are you?"

I can see Evie's jaw tighten, her patience wearing thin. "I'm someone who cares about her," she says, her voice low and controlled. "Now leave. She doesn't want you here."

The moment hangs in the air, tense and brittle, and I want to pull Evie back, tell her to let it go, that I can handle this. But Gareth's eyes flicker with something dark, and his lips curl into a bitter smile.

"You don't even know, do you?" he says, laughing under

his breath. "You think you know her? You don't know the half of it."

Evie's expression hardens, but I can see the confusion creeping in. She glances at me, and I can't meet her eyes. I feel exposed, like all the walls I've built around this part of my life are crumbling, and there's nothing I can do to stop it.

"Who are you?" Evie asks, her voice edged with anger and a hint of fear.

Gareth doesn't miss a beat. He looks straight at Evie, and when he speaks, his words are like a punch to the gut, knocking the air out of my lungs.

"I'm her husband."

Evie's eyes widen, and she takes a step back, the shock of his words hitting her like a wave. She turns to me, searching my face for some kind of explanation, and all I can see in her eyes is hurt and confusion. My stomach twists, a sickening mix of shame and panic, and suddenly everything feels like it's spiraling out of control.

"Sasha," she whispers, her voice cracking, "is that true?"

I open my mouth to speak, to say anything, but the words get stuck, tangled in the mess of everything I've been trying to keep hidden. I feel the world closing in, the weight of Gareth's presence, the betrayal in Evie's eyes, and for a moment, I'm not sure what to do. The truth is out, and it feels like the ground has just been ripped out from under me.

This isn't how it was supposed to go. This isn't how Evie was supposed to find out. But now, standing in the cold, empty street, with Gareth smirking at me and Evie's hurt gaze piercing through, I realize I can't run from this anymore. I slowly nod.

17

EVIE

I'm already smiling as I approach the restaurant, the neon glow of Bourbon Wings spilling onto the sidewalk and lighting up the faces of the lingering customers and passersby. I've been looking forward to seeing Sasha all day, imagining the way she always lights up when she spots me, the easy grin she saves just for us when we're alone. It's been a long shift, I know, but we've got the rest of the night, and I can't wait to fall back into the comfort of our routine—wine on the couch, her laugh filling the room, and the world feeling a little brighter just because she's in it.

But as I get closer, I see Sasha standing outside, her shoulders tense, her face half-turned away from the entrance. She's not alone. There's a man with her, tall and sharp-featured, his posture relaxed, but there's something coiled in the way he stands that makes my stomach knot. He's handsome in an obvious, deliberate way—dark hair perfectly styled, clothes that scream money without being flashy. He's got that kind of effortless arrogance, the look of someone who's used to being listened to, obeyed. It sets my teeth on edge before I' even hear him speak.

The way Sasha's holding herself tells me everything. She's rigid, her hands balled into fists at her sides, her expression tight and guarded. I can't hear what they're saying, but I don't need to; it's written all over her face—she's scared, trapped, and I can't stand to see her like that.

I move closer, my footsteps echoing in the quiet street, and I call out, trying to sound casual but knowing I'm anything but. "Sasha, everything okay?"

She turns, her eyes widening when she sees me, and there's a flash of relief that quickly dims into something else, something that makes my heart drop. The man shifts his gaze to me, assessing, and his expression flickers with mild annoyance, like I'm nothing more than an interruption. His presence radiates confidence, but not the good kind; it's smug and calculated, the kind that makes me want to keep my distance.

"This doesn't concern you," he says flatly, his voice low and clipped, like he's barely bothered to acknowledge me. There's an English accent, smooth and cold, and it fits him.

I step closer, ignoring the warning in his tone. "She's asked you to leave," I say, keeping my voice steady even though my pulse is thrumming in my ears. "So why don't you do that?"

He straightens, crossing his arms, and for a second, I can't help but notice how effortlessly he commands attention. He's the kind of man you'd spot in a room full of people—self-assured, sharp-eyed, with a presence that demands space. Everything about him exudes control, from the expensive cut of his jacket to the way he holds himself, like he owns the ground he's standing on.

"And who the hell are you?" he asks, a faint smirk tugging at the corner of his mouth. He's looking at me like I'm some minor inconvenience, an obstacle he can brush aside, and it makes my blood simmer.

"I'm someone who cares about her," I say, trying to keep my temper in check. "Now leave. She doesn't want you here."

There's a tense silence, and I can feel Sasha beside me, tight as a wire, caught between us. I want to pull her away, to put myself between her and this man, but she's frozen, her eyes darting between us as if she's weighing every possible outcome.

The man—Gareth, I think she called him—lets out a short, humorless laugh. "You don't even know, do you?" he says, his tone dripping with condescension. "You think you know her? You don't know the half of it."

I glance at Sasha, my heart pounding, trying to read the panic in her eyes. She looks at me like she's about to speak, but no words come. I turn back to him, my anger bubbling to the surface. "Who are you?" I demand, each word laced with growing fear. "Who the hell do you think you are?"

He doesn't hesitate, doesn't blink. He just looks straight at me with a cold, knowing smile. "I'm her husband."

The words land like a punch, stealing the breath from my lungs. I blink, trying to process what he's just said, but the ground beneath me feels like it's shifted. Husband. It's a word I've never associated with Sasha, something I've never even considered. My mind scrambles for any piece of information that makes sense of this, but all I see is Sasha—her wide eyes, her trembling hands, the tightness in her posture.

I turn to her, searching her face for something, anything that will prove him wrong. But she doesn't say a word. She just stares back at me, her eyes glossy and filled with something I can't quite name—fear, guilt, maybe even shame. It's the confirmation I don't want, the answer I've been dreading in the seconds since he spoke, and it hits me harder than I thought possible.

"Sasha," I whisper, my voice cracking as I try to hold onto the thread of everything I thought I knew. "Is that true?"

She doesn't need to say it. Her silence is enough. She nods, a small, barely perceptible motion, but it's like the final blow, knocking the wind out of me completely. I feel my chest tighten, the sharp sting of betrayal cutting through the haze. I can't breathe. I can't think. I just need to get out of here.

Without another word, I turn on my heel and walk away, each step feeling heavier than the last. My vision blurs, and all I can hear is the rush of blood in my ears drowning out everything else. I don't look back. I can't. I just keep moving, putting distance between me and the truth that's unraveling everything I thought I knew about Sasha, about us.

I need to be anywhere but here. Away from the man who claims to own a piece of her, away from the look in Sasha's eyes that I can't bear to face. My heart pounds as I round the corner, the city lights blinking above me, indifferent to the storm that's just ripped through my chest. I feel sick and disoriented, but I don't stop. I can't stop.

All I know is that I need to be alone, to make sense of this, to figure out how the woman I've been falling for has been hiding a whole life from me. A husband. The word echoes in my mind, each repetition twisting the knife deeper.

I don't know what to think. I don't know how to feel. All I

know is that I've been blindsided, and the Sasha I thought I knew feels nonexistent.

∼

I don't know how I make it to the bookstore. My legs feel like they're moving on their own, one foot in front of the other without any real sense of direction. I'm numb, the world around me a blur of headlights and passing faces. The voices on the street are muffled, blending into the hum of the city, but I can't focus on anything except the thudding in my chest and the endless loop of Gareth's voice ringing in my ears.

I'm her husband.

The words keep echoing, loud and sharp, tearing through the thin veneer of calm I've been trying to maintain. I push through the heavy wooden door of the bookstore, the familiar creak of the hinges barely registering. I lock it behind me, flicking the sign to "closed," even though it's late and no one would be coming in anyway. It's reflexive, automatic, like I need to shut myself away from the world to keep out everything that's unraveling around me.

The store is dark except for the faint light filtering in from the streetlamps outside that are casting long shadows across the shelves. Usually, this place feels like home—a haven of paper and ink, the smell of old books wrapping around me like a warm hug. But tonight, the shadows feel heavier, like they're closing in, and I can't find the comfort I usually do here. The quiet feels oppressive, pressing against my ears, amplifying the storm in my head.

I move through the aisles without purpose, just wandering, my fingers brushing the spines of books that have always been there, constant and dependable. My mind is racing, but everything feels distant and disconnected, like I'm floating outside of myself. I keep seeing Sasha's face, the way she looked at me when Gareth spoke—the guilt, the fear, the silent apology in her eyes that I didn't understand until now.

I reach the poetry section, the heart of the store where Sasha and I have spent so many nights together. I sink to the floor, leaning back against the shelves, and close my eyes, trying to ground myself in the familiar scent of old pages and dust. But every time I try to focus, all I see is Gareth standing there, tall and arrogant, his words slicing through the air like a knife.

How could she keep this from me? How could she let me fall for her without ever mentioning something so huge? A husband. It's like a foreign concept, a word that feels too big, too final, too completely wrong for the Sasha I thought I knew.

I pull my knees to my chest, feeling small and overwhelmed, and let out a shaky breath. The bookstore has always been my refuge, but tonight, it feels different. The walls seem closer, the air heavier. I've built my whole life here—sheltered by stories and words that never hurt me, never lied to me. But now, everything feels tainted. I think of all the times Sasha and I sat here, laughing and talking as if nothing else existed. How much of that was real? How much of it was just another lie?

I rub my hands over my face, trying to shake the suffocating feeling. I want to scream, to cry, to do something that will make this heaviness lift, but all I can manage is a series of shallow breaths, each one more labored than the last. I pull a book off the shelf—an old poetry collection I've read a dozen times—and flip through the pages, but the words blur together, meaningless in the mess of my thoughts.

I can't believe I let this happen. I've been so careful, so guarded with my heart ever since... I swallow, refusing to let myself go there. But Sasha slipped in so easily, so effortlessly, and now it's like I'm falling backward into a place I promised myself I'd never go again. I thought I was smarter, stronger, but here I am, blindsided by someone I let get too close.

I reach into my bag, pulling out my journal, the one I keep hidden behind the counter. It's my go-to when things get too heavy, my place to let it all out without judgment. I flip it open to a blank page, the pen trembling in my hand as I press it to the paper. The words spill out messily and unfiltered, driven by the anger and hurt twisting inside me.

How could she lie? How could I be so stupid? I thought I knew her, but now I see I've been looking at a stranger. I don't even know who I've been letting into my life, into my heart.

I keep writing, the ink smearing as tears blur my vision. It's ugly, and it doesn't make me feel better, but it's something. The anger is easier to handle than the sadness and betrayal that sit like a heavy stone in my chest. I don't know what hurts more: the fact that she didn't tell me or the realization that she's been hiding this whole part of herself from me all along.

I thought I was safe with her. I thought we were building something real, something that wasn't tangled up in secrets. But now it's all tainted, every kiss, every whispered promise. I flip back through the pages of my journal, reading old entries that now feel naïve, too hopeful. Sasha was always there, woven into every line, every reflection on the future I was starting to imagine. And now, it's like those words don't belong to me anymore; they belong to the version of us that never really existed.

I slam the journal shut, frustration bubbling up as I toss it aside. My eyes dart around the bookstore, searching for something to hold on to, something to ground me, but all I see are reminders of what I've lost. The poetry section where she'd pull out books and read to me, her voice low and soft. The coffee bar where she'd lean against the counter, teasing me about my overly complicated drink orders. The corner where we'd curl up together sharing secret smiles as we read late into the night. It all feels tainted now, stained by the truth that was lurking just beneath the surface.

I stand up, feeling restless, trapped in a space that's supposed to be my sanctuary. I need air, something to clear my head, but the thought of going outside, of being anywhere that isn't here, is too much. I just need to figure this out, to make sense of how I went from feeling like I'd found something real to standing on the edge of a precipice about to lose it all.

I pace between the shelves, trying to push the anger back, but it keeps clawing its way up. I want to confront her, to demand answers, but I'm terrified of what she might say, terrified of hearing that everything we had was built on a lie. I don't know how to face that. I don't know if I'm strong enough.

Eventually, I find myself back in the poetry section, my favorite corner of the store. I pull a book off the shelf—one of my most treasured collections—and open it to a page I've read a hundred times before. The words are familiar, comforting in their repetition, but tonight, they feel different, like they're mocking me with their promises of love and honesty. I slam it shut, the sound echoing in the empty store.

I can't stay here. Not like this. I can't keep replaying everything in my head, turning it over and over, looking for answers that aren't there. I need space. I need time to think, to figure out what I want, what I need. I think about Sasha's face when she nodded, the way her eyes filled with a kind of sadness that almost broke me. She's hurting too—I know that—but right now, I can't see past my own pain.

I pull out my phone, opening a new message to Sasha, my fingers hovering over the keyboard. I type and delete, type and delete, the words never feeling right. I want to ask her why. I want to yell at her, to make her understand how much she's hurt me, but I can't bring myself to send anything. I'm not ready to talk, not ready to hear whatever excuse she might have.

So, I turn off my phone, sliding it into my bag, and take a deep breath, forcing myself to slow down. I need to set boundaries, to figure out where I stand before I can face her again. She's kept so much from me, and I can't let myself be dragged into the chaos of her past. Not until I know I'm ready.

I make a decision then, quiet and resolute: I'm taking a step back. I need to protect myself, to protect this space that I've built, this life that is mine. I need to figure out who I am without Sasha wrapped up in every thought, every plan. I don't know what comes next, but I know I need time to breathe, to heal, to decide if I can forgive her or if this is the end.

I pick up the poetry book from the floor, tucking it back onto the shelf with a heavy heart. The store is quiet again, the shadows long and soft, and I let myself sink into the silence. It's not the peace I was hoping for, but it's something. I stand there for a long time, surrounded by the books that have always been my constant, and slowly, the storm inside me starts to settle.

I know I can't hide here forever, but for tonight, it's enough. I take a seat on the floor, my back against the shelves, and close my eyes, letting the quiet wash over me. Tomorrow, I'll face whatever comes. But tonight, I'm here, and that's all I can manage.

18

SASHA

The street is nearly empty, the last of the wing shop customers having drifted away, and it's just me and Gareth now, standing under the flickering glow of the streetlamp. Evie's gone, and the space she left behind feels like a gaping wound, raw and exposed. I watch her disappear down the street, my chest tight with a mix of anger, guilt, and fear. I want to run after her, to make her understand, but my feet stay glued to the pavement. I'm stuck here, facing the one person I hoped I'd never have to see again.

Gareth leans casually against the brick wall, his posture relaxed but his eyes sharp, the same calculating gaze I've spent years trying to forget. He looks at me like he's got the upper hand, and maybe he does. He's tall, dressed in a tailored coat that probably cost more than my month's rent, and has this infuriating air of confidence, like he owns every room he walks into. He's handsome in that polished, put-together way, but all I see is the arrogance and entitlement that comes with money and privilege.

"What the hell are you doing here, Gareth?" I snap, my

voice shaky but edged with the anger that's been building since he showed up. "I told you to leave me alone."

Gareth straightens, brushing imaginary dust off his coat, and I can see the faint smirk tugging at his lips. "I didn't come here to argue, Sasha. I came to get what I need so I can finally put this mess behind me."

I take a step back, crossing my arms defensively, trying to keep the distance between us. "What mess? You were the one who pushed this, remember? You were the one who wouldn't take no for an answer."

He rolls his eyes, a dismissive gesture that makes my blood boil. "We've been over this. You're not some innocent victim here. You said yes, Sasha. You said yes, and then you ran."

The words sting, and I hate that he's right, at least about the running part. I did say yes, but not because I wanted to. I said yes because it was easier than fighting, easier than standing up to everyone who told me it was the right thing to do. Gareth's family had pulled strings, and I was the girl from the wrong side of the tracks who got caught up in something I never wanted. The marriage was just another deal to them, something to be managed and controlled, and I'd been too scared and too young to push back.

"I never wanted any of it," I say, my voice breaking. "I never wanted you, or the life you were trying to make me live. I left because I couldn't breathe. I left because you and your family pushed me into something I didn't want."

He shakes his head, his expression darkening. "And you think I did? You think this was my dream? I was as trapped as you were, Sasha. But I didn't just disappear. I didn't just leave you to clean up the mess."

I flinch, the guilt crashing over me. He's right about that too. The way I left wasn't fair, or right, but I'd felt cornered, suffocated by the weight of everyone else's expectations. I packed a bag one night, booked the first flight I could find, and never looked back. I didn't tell anyone, didn't say goodbye. I just needed out, and I didn't care what bridges I had to burn to get there.

"I'm sorry," I say, and it feels hollow, too little, too late. "I know I left you in a bad place, but we both know we were never meant to be together. It was a mistake from the start."

Gareth sighs, his expression shifting from anger to something that almost looks like resignation. "I know that now," he admits, and it's the first time I've heard him sound anything other than smug or bitter. "I don't want you back, Sasha. I'm not here to drag you back into my life. I've moved on, or at least I'm trying to."

I blink, caught off guard. It's not the response I was expecting, and for a second, the fight drains out of me. "Then why are you here?" I ask, my voice quieter now, the edge softening.

He reaches into his coat pocket and pulls out an envelope, holding it out to me. "I need you to sign the divorce papers. It's the last thing tying us together, and I can't move forward until it's done. I've tried to get them to you, but you've been impossible to find."

I stare at the envelope, the weight of it heavy in his hand. It feels like a symbol of everything I've been avoiding, the final severing of the life I left behind. I take it from him hesitantly, my fingers brushing against the crisp paper, and for a moment, I feel the full gravity of what this means. This isn't just about ending a marriage I never wanted; it's about letting go of the guilt, the shame, and the fear that's been haunting me since the day I left.

"You really don't want me back?" I ask, needing to hear it

one more time, needing to know that this is about more than just ending a contract.

Gareth shakes his head, his expression unreadable. "No, Sasha. I don't want you. I just want my life back, and I need you to let me have that. We're not kids anymore. We're not trapped. Let's just end this and go our separate ways."

I nod, swallowing hard. It's so simple, the way he says it, but it feels monumental, like the final chapter of a book I've been stuck in for too long. "I'll sign them," I say, my voice steadier now. "But you need to understand—leaving was the only way I knew how to save myself. I'm sorry for the way I did it, but I don't regret getting out."

Gareth studies me, and for the first time, I think he really sees me, sees the person I've become outside of the life we were forced into. "I get it," he says finally, and there's a softness in his tone that I've never heard before. "Just...don't disappear on anyone else, okay? It's not fair to keep running."

He turns to leave, and I watch him walk away, the tension in my shoulders slowly easing. It's not closure, not entirely, but it's something. I look down at the envelope in my hand, feeling lighter, like I've finally cut one of the strings that's been pulling me back.

∽

By the time I make it to Glass's place, my mind is spinning with everything that's just happened. I need to talk to someone, to get this mess out of my head, and Glass is the only person who knows enough to help me make sense of it all. He's sprawled on his couch, a half-empty bottle of red wine on the table, and he raises an eyebrow when he sees me, reading my expression before I even say a word.

"Rough night?" he asks, his tone teasing but tinged with concern. Glass always knows when I'm on the edge, and tonight, I'm dangling by a thread.

"You could say that," I mutter, sinking into the armchair opposite him. I pull the divorce papers out of my bag and toss them onto the table, the sight of them making my stomach twist. "Gareth showed up."

Glass's eyes widen, and he sets his wine down, suddenly serious. "What the hell? I thought you got away from all that."

"I did. Or at least I thought I did," I say, running a hand through my hair in frustration. "He found me. And he told Evie. She...she knows everything now. Or at least the worst parts."

Glass lets out a low whistle, leaning back and crossing his arms. "Well, shit. I'm guessing that didn't go over well."

"No, it didn't," I admit, the weight of it sinking in all over again. "She walked away. I tried to tell her it wasn't what it looked like, but Gareth just had to drop the bomb before I could say anything."

"What does he want?" Glass asks, nodding toward the papers on the table.

"Just for me to sign the damn papers," I say, my voice heavy with exhaustion. "He's done. I'm done. But he showed up at the worst possible time, and now Evie... I don't know how to fix this."

Glass is quiet for a moment, studying me with those sharp eyes that miss nothing. "You've got to tell her the whole story, Sash. The running, the marriage, everything. You can't keep piecing it out and expecting her to understand. She's hurt. And you hiding this didn't help."

"I know," I say, and it's like admitting it makes it hurt all the more. "I just...I was scared, okay? I didn't want to scare her off with my baggage. I thought if I could just keep moving forward, maybe it wouldn't matter."

Glass gives me a sympathetic smile, reaching across to squeeze my hand. "But it does matter. And if you really care about her, you owe her the truth. All of it. Not just the parts you think she wants to hear."

I nod, feeling the sting of his words but knowing he's right. "I don't want to lose her, Glass. She's everything I didn't think I could have."

"Then don't lose her," he says simply. "Fight for her. Show her that you're willing to be honest, even if it's messy and painful. You can't control how she reacts, but at least you'll know you gave it your all."

I look at the divorce papers again, the final piece of a chapter that's haunted me for too long. Glass is right. If I want a future with Evie, I have to confront the past, not just run from it. I have to be willing to stand still, to be seen, even when it hurts.

I pick up my phone, staring at Evie's name in my contacts, my thumb hovering over the call button. I'm terrified, but I know I have to try. I have to tell her everything and hope that it's not too late.

"Thanks, Glass," I say, my voice steadier now, filled with a quiet resolve. "I'm going to make this right. I have to."

He raises his glass in a mock toast, his smile warm and encouraging. "You've got this, Sash. Now go get your girl."

I nod, my heart pounding with fear and determination. I don't know if Evie will forgive me, but I know one thing: I'm done running. It's time to fight for the life I want, the one I deserve. And that starts with facing Evie. No more secrets, no more lies. Just the truth, however messy it may be.

19

EVIE

I haven't been able to shake the hollow feeling that's been gnawing at me since last night. The bookstore is supposed to be my sanctuary, but this morning, it feels more like a prison. I've been here for hours already, but I can't remember a single thing I've done. There's a pile of books to shelve, but they just sit in a messy stack by the counter. My hands move automatically, straightening things here and there, but nothing feels real. Not after last night. Not after what *he* said.

I keep replaying his words in my head, over and over. *I'm her husband.* It's like a hammer, each repetition driving a nail deeper into my heart. How could she not tell me? How could she keep something like that hidden from me? I didn't even know she was bisexual. Or straight? Or whatever she identifies as. Am I her first relationship with a woman?

Not that it matters, really. But I thought I knew her. I knew she had secrets, sure, and I never wanted to pry. But I never ever suspected a husband.

I glance around the store, trying to focus on the familiar

surroundings, hoping the comfort of these walls will pull me out of this fog. The smell of old paper, the quiet murmur of the city outside—it's usually enough to settle me, to remind me that everything will be okay. But today, it feels distant, like I'm disconnected from the life I've built here.

The bell above the door rings, breaking the silence. I look up and see Kenneth strolling in, his usual bright smile in place as he waves at me from across the store. He's carrying two cups of coffee, and the sight of him with those ridiculous pink-framed glasses perched on his nose makes me want to cry for some reason.

"Morning, boss," he says cheerfully, crossing the room in a few long strides. "I brought caffeine. Figured you might need it after staying late last night."

I manage a weak smile, though it feels more like a grimace. "Thanks, Kenneth. I...I do need it." My voice sounds fragile, thin.

He sets the coffee down in front of me and leans against the counter, his eyes narrowing as he studies me. "Okay, what's going on? You look like you haven't slept in weeks. And I mean more than the usual 'I'm running a bookstore and never have time to rest' look."

I laugh, but it's humorless, barely a sound. "I didn't sleep much, no."

He raises an eyebrow, waiting for me to say more, but I can't. Not yet. The words are stuck, lodged somewhere between my chest and my throat. I take a long sip of the coffee, hoping the warmth will soothe the ache inside me, but it doesn't.

Kenneth doesn't move, just stays there, leaning on the counter like he's got all the time in the world. He's not the pushy type, but he knows when something's wrong. It's one of the reasons I hired him. He's good with people, good with me.

"Evie," he says, his voice soft but insistent. "What's going on? You've got that look like you're about to either break down or throw a book at someone's head."

I exhale sharply, setting the cup down with a thud. "It's Sasha."

Kenneth's expression shifts, his teasing smile fading as concern takes over. "What happened? Did you guys have a fight?"

I shake my head, feeling the sting of tears at the edges of my vision. "No, not exactly. She...she's been hiding something from me. Something big."

He straightens, folding his arms across his chest as he listens, giving me the space to find the words.

"She is married," I say, the words spilling out before I can stop them. "She never told me. Her husband—ex-husband, whatever he is—he showed up last night. At the restaurant. And he told me."

Kenneth's eyes widens. "Wait, what? Sasha's married?"

"I mean I don't think they are still together. She spends all her time with me. But clearly they were," I say, feeling the bitterness creep into my voice. "She didn't bother to tell me that part. He just dropped it like a bomb, right in front of me. And she just stood there, like...like she was waiting for the world to fall apart."

Kenneth runs a hand through his hair, clearly trying to process what I've just told him. "Damn, Evie. That's a lot."

I nod, swallowing the lump in my throat. "Yeah, it is. And I don't know what to do with it. I feel like I don't even know her. Like everything we've had is built on a lie."

He reaches out, placing a hand on mine. "You deserve

honesty, Evie. You deserve someone who's upfront with you from the start. This sounds like a huge betrayal."

I feel a tear slip down my cheek before I can stop it. "I just don't understand why she didn't tell me. I gave her so many chances to open up, to trust me. And now, after everything, I don't know if I can trust her at all."

Kenneth squeezes my hand, his eyes full of empathy. "Look, I'm not going to tell you what to do here. But maybe she was scared. I mean, hiding something that big...she must have been terrified of what it would do to your relationship."

I laugh bitterly, wiping at my eyes. "Well, it's done plenty. She's gone now, and I'm left here, trying to figure out what the hell is real anymore."

He lets out a long breath, giving me a look that's both compassionate and firm. "You don't have to figure it all out right now. Take some time, Evie. Let yourself feel everything, and then decide what you want. You deserve to take the time you need to process this."

I nod, but the weight of his words only seems to press down harder on me. "I'm scared, Kenneth. I'm scared that I'll never be able to look at her the same way again. And I don't want to lose her, but...I don't know if I can forgive this."

Kenneth is quiet for a moment, and when he speaks, his voice is soft but steady. "Whatever happens, just remember that you deserve someone who is honest with you. You don't have to settle for less, even if it hurts to let go."

I bite my lip, blinking back more tears. "I know. I just... I thought we had something real."

He squeezes my hand one last time before letting go. "Maybe you still do, but that's for you to figure out. And you don't have to figure it out today."

I nod, feeling a little lighter now that I've said it all out loud. The tightness in my chest hasn't disappeared, but at least I'm not carrying it alone anymore.

"I'm going to shelve some books," I say, needing to distract myself for a little while.

Kenneth gives me a reassuring smile. "I'll take over the counter for a bit. Take your time."

∼

I find myself back in the poetry section. It's where Sasha and I spent so many evenings curled up with books, sharing quiet moments that felt like they were ours alone. Now it feels different. Every corner of the store is filled with her, with memories that I'm not sure I can trust anymore.

I glance at the stack of notebooks on one of the tables, the ones Sasha left here. Her poetry. Her words.

I hesitate, my fingers hovering over the cover of the top notebook. Part of me doesn't want to read it. What if the words feel hollow now? What if everything she wrote was as much a lie as the life she kept hidden from me?

But then I pick it up, unable to help myself. I open to the first page, my eyes scanning the familiar lines of her handwriting. It's a poem I've read before, one she shared with me the night we first kissed. It's about love, about trust, about building something beautiful out of fragile moments.

We build our walls with fragile care,
Thin as glass, they're always there.
A single look, a fleeting glance,
Can break them down with just a chance.

The words hit me differently now. I'd thought it was about us, about the way we were slowly opening up to each other, letting our walls come down. But now, I wonder if it was about her, about the walls she was keeping up all along.

I flip through more pages, reading poems I've never seen before. Some are about love, others about fear, about hiding, about running. The lines blur together as I read, my heart aching with every verse. I'm searching for something, for some clue, some explanation that will make it all make sense. But all I find are more questions.

How much of this was about me? How much of it was about her past, the life she never told me about?

I close the notebook, feeling the weight of it in my hands. The words are beautiful, but they're also haunting. They make me realize just how much I don't know about Sasha, how much she's kept hidden behind her poetry.

I sit down at the small table, the one where we used to sit together, and I let the silence wash over me. I want to understand her, to believe that there's more to her than the secrets she kept. But I don't know if I can. I don't know if I can separate the woman I fell for from the lies she told.

As I sit there, lost in thought, the bell above the door rings again. I don't look up right away, but then I hear a familiar voice—soft, hesitant.

"Evie?"

I freeze, my heart lurching in my chest. I know that voice.

I know it too well.

Slowly, I lift my head, and there she is—Sasha, standing just inside the doorway, her lovely green eyes wide with uncertainty. She looks nervous, like she's not sure if she should be here, but there's something else in her expression too. A kind of desperation, like she's here because she has no other choice.

"Can we talk?" she asks, her voice barely above a whisper.

I don't know what to say. The words stick in my throat, tangled with the anger and hurt that's still fresh, still raw.

But I nod, because even though I'm still furious, I need answers. I need to know why she did this. Why she kept this part of her life hidden from me.

Sasha steps forward, her eyes never leaving mine. And as she moves closer, I realize that whatever happens next, nothing between us will ever be the same.

20

SASHA

I walk toward the bookstore, every step heavier than the last. My heart feels like it's caught in a vise, the pressure building with every block. I can see the familiar storefront ahead, but the thought of going inside makes my stomach twist. I don't know if I have the right words for Evie. How do I explain why I hid something so big, why I kept my past locked away like some shameful secret?

The truth is, I've been running for so long I'm not sure I know how to stop.

As I get closer, the memories creep in, memories I've been trying to push down for years. They hit me all at once, images of the day I left Gareth. The moment everything fell apart.

I hadn't planned on leaving that night. It just...happened.

I'd been standing in the hallway of our house, my fingers wrapped around the handle of a suitcase I'd barely packed. My heart was racing, the weight of everything pressing down on me, making it hard to breathe. Gareth was in the other room, sitting in front of the TV like

The Words of Us 183

nothing was wrong, like our life wasn't crumbling around us.

"I can't do this anymore," I had whispered to myself, my voice trembling.

But the truth was, I'd been saying that for months, over and over in my head, trapped in a life that never felt like mine. The marriage, the house, the expectations—it was all something I'd been pushed into. I never wanted to marry Gareth. I never wanted to be someone's perfect wife, but I said yes because it was easier than saying no, easier than fighting the inevitable. His family, my family, the pressure—it all wrapped around me, pulling me into a role I never asked for.

I remember standing in the doorway of the living room, watching him, trying to find the words. My mouth was dry, and my hands were shaking as I gripped the suitcase tighter.

"Gareth," I said, my voice breaking the silence.

He didn't look up from the TV, just gave a dismissive grunt. "What is it, Sasha?"

I took a deep breath, feeling the tightness in my chest, the fear and the guilt swirling together. "I'm leaving."

That got his attention. He turned slowly, his eyes narrowing in confusion. "What do you mean, leaving?"

"I mean I can't stay here anymore," I said, my voice stronger than I felt. "I can't keep pretending this is what I want."

His expression darkened, the confusion replaced with a hard, cold anger. He stood up, crossing the room toward me, his presence filling the space like a storm cloud. "You're not making any sense. We're married, Sasha. This is your life. You don't just walk out because things get tough."

"I didn't want this," I shot back, my voice shaking now. "I never wanted this. You pushed me into it. Your family, mine

—they decided everything for me. But I can't keep living like this. I'm suffocating."

Gareth's jaw clenched, his hands balling into fists at his sides. "We made a commitment. You can't just leave because you're feeling trapped. That's not how this works."

Tears burned at the corners of my eyes, but I forced them back, refusing to let him see how scared I was. "You don't understand. I've been trapped since the day I said yes. This marriage—it's not real. It's just... it's just something we did because it was expected."

He stared at me for a long moment, his eyes hard and unyielding. "So, what? You're just going to run away? You think that's going to fix everything?"

I didn't have an answer. All I knew was that staying was slowly killing me. Every day in that house, every moment in that life that wasn't mine—it was too much. I wasn't Sasha anymore. I was someone else, someone who lived for other people, for their expectations and their plans. And I couldn't do it anymore.

"I'm sorry," I whispered, my voice breaking as the guilt finally hit me. "I'm sorry for the way I'm doing this, but I have to go."

He didn't say anything, just stood there, staring at me with a mixture of anger and disbelief. And in that moment, I felt the weight of it all—the guilt, the fear, the shame of leaving without a proper goodbye. But I couldn't stay. Staying would've meant losing myself completely.

I turned, pulling the door open, and as I stepped outside into the cool night air, I felt the tears finally spill over. I didn't look back. I couldn't. I just kept walking, leaving everything behind—the house, the marriage, the person I had been pretending to be.

Now, as I stand outside the bookstore, the memory feels like a fresh wound, raw and aching. I left Gareth because I had to. I didn't know how else to save myself. But I never told Evie about that part of my life, and now it's come back to haunt me. And the worst part is, I can't even say I regret leaving. I regret how I left, but not the leaving itself. It was the only way I knew how to breathe again.

But Evie deserves more than that. She deserves the truth, all of it, no matter how much it hurts.

I push open the door to the bookstore, the bell above the door ringing softly. The familiar scent of books and coffee hits me, but it doesn't bring the comfort it usually does. Instead, it feels heavy, like a reminder of everything that's at stake.

Evie's sitting at a small table near the back, surrounded by books and papers, her back to the door. For a moment, I just watch her, my heart pounding. She looks tired, like she hasn't slept, and I know that's my fault. I did this to her. I kept the truth from her, and now she's paying the price.

I take a deep breath and step forward, my voice barely above a whisper. "Evie?"

She freezes, her shoulders tensing, and slowly turns to face me. Her eyes are red, like she's been crying, and the sight of it breaks something inside me.

"Sasha," she says, her voice flat, emotionless. "What are you doing here?"

"I...I need to talk to you," I say, my voice trembling. "I need to explain."

She doesn't say anything, just watches me, waiting. The silence between us feels like a chasm, wide and impossible to cross. But I have to try.

"I'm sorry," I start, the words falling out in a rush. "I should've told you about Gareth. I should've been honest with you from the beginning. But I was scared. I was scared of losing you, scared that if you knew about my past, you wouldn't want me anymore."

Evie's expression doesn't change. She just listens, her eyes hard, unreadable.

"I left him," I continue, my voice shaking. "I left because I couldn't breathe in that life. I never wanted to marry him, but I felt like I didn't have a choice. Our families...they pushed me into it, and I was too weak to fight back. But it wasn't real. None of it was real."

Evie's eyes flicker, but she doesn't say anything.

"I'm not asking for your forgiveness," I say, my voice cracking. "I know I messed up. I should've told you the truth, but I didn't know how. And now...now I'm terrified that I've ruined everything."

I look at her, desperate for some kind of response, some sign that she understands. But she just sits there staring at me, her expression unreadable.

"Why didn't you tell me?" she finally asks, her voice quiet but sharp, like a knife slicing through the air. "Why did you keep something like that from me?"

"Because I didn't want you to look at me differently," I whisper, my throat tight with emotion. "I didn't want you to see me as someone with baggage, someone who's broken. I wanted to be the person you deserved, and I thought that if I told you about Gareth, it would ruin everything."

Evie's lips press into a thin line, and she shakes her head slowly. "You think this is about me seeing you as broken? It's about trust, Sasha. How am I supposed to trust you if you keep hiding things from me?"

The words hit me like a punch to the gut, and I feel tears

prick at my eyes. "I know," I whisper. "I know I broke your trust, and I hate myself for it. But I'm here now, telling you everything because I can't keep running from this. I don't want to run anymore."

She doesn't respond right away, and the silence stretches between us, heavy and suffocating.

"I need time," she finally says, her voice tight with emotion. "I need time to figure out if I can forgive this. Because right now, I don't know."

The words are like a knife in my chest, but I nod, swallowing back the tears. "I understand. Take all the time you need."

I stand in the bookstore, the silence stretching between us like an unspoken question. I've said everything I could, laid it all out in front of her. There's no going back now. The words are out there, hanging in the air, and I can't take them back. I wouldn't, even if I could. For once, I've stopped running. I've stopped hiding.

But I can't shake the sinking feeling in my stomach. I've hurt her. That much is clear from the way she looks at me; her eyes are full of hurt and confusion, and I know I'm the cause of that. Part of me wants to beg her to forgive me, to promise that I'll never lie again, that I'll do anything to fix this. But I don't. I can't.

I can't control what happens next.

"Evie," I say quietly, my voice breaking the stillness. She looks up at me, her expression unreadable, and my heart aches. "I'm not going to run from this anymore. I'll be here when you're ready—if you're ready. I just need you to know that no matter what happens, I'm grateful for the time we've had together. Even if it's over."

The words are harder to say than I thought they'd be. Admitting that I might lose her feels like ripping out a piece of myself, but I can't keep holding onto something I don't have control over. I can't make her forgive me. All I can do is give her the space to decide for herself.

Evie watches me, her lips pressing into a thin line, and for a moment, I wonder if she'll say something, anything. But she stays quiet, and I understand. She needs time to process all of this. I can't push her.

So, I take a deep breath, giving her one last look, trying to hold onto the memory of what we've shared, just in case this is the end.

"I'll go," I say softly. "But if you ever want to talk, I'll be here."

With that, I turn and walk toward the door, my heart heavy with the weight of everything unsaid. My hand hovers over the doorknob for a second, but I don't look back. I can't. I open the door, stepping out into the cold evening air, feeling the finality of the moment settle over me.

I've done all I can. The rest is up to her.

∼

The cold hits me as soon as I step outside, a sharp contrast to the warmth of the bookstore. I pull my coat tighter around me, my breath fogging in the air as I walk down the street, my feet moving without direction. The city around me feels distant, like I'm watching it from the outside, disconnected from the noise and the bustle. Everything is muffled, like I'm trapped in my own world, my thoughts louder than anything else.

I don't know what I expected. I poured my heart out to Evie, told her everything, but now I'm left with nothing but uncertainty. I don't know if she'll ever forgive me, and the thought of losing her—of losing what we've built together—

it feels like I'm standing on the edge of a cliff, waiting to see if I'll fall.

But for the first time in a long time, I'm not hiding. I'm not running. I told her the truth, and that should bring me some sense of relief. And in a way, it does. I'm not carrying the weight of my secret anymore. The truth is out there, and it's no longer gnawing at me from the inside. But the relief is mixed with a deep, gnawing fear. I know that the truth doesn't fix everything. It doesn't erase the hurt I've caused.

I stop in front of a small park, the trees bare and the grass frosted over. The benches are empty, and the quietness of the scene pulls me in. I sit down, my legs suddenly feeling heavy, like the exhaustion of everything is finally catching up to me.

The memories of the past few weeks with Evie flood my mind. The way she smiled at me that first night at the poetry reading, the sound of her laugh, the way she looked at me like I was something good, something worth holding onto. And now I've shattered that trust, that connection.

I close my eyes, leaning back against the bench, trying to push back the tears that threaten to spill over. I didn't want it to end like this. I didn't want to hurt her, but I did. I know that I can't undo what I've done, but I hope, deep down, that maybe she can still see the good in us. That maybe she can find it in her heart to forgive me.

But the uncertainty of it all—it's crushing. I've never been good at waiting, at sitting with the unknown. I've always been the one to make decisions, to act before thinking. But now, all I can do is wait. And it's terrifying.

I take a deep breath, letting the cold air fill my lungs, trying to calm the storm in my mind. The city lights flicker in the distance as cars pass by, life moving forward around me. But I'm stuck here, frozen in this moment, waiting to see if Evie will catch me or let me fall.

I think about going back to my apartment, but the idea of sitting there alone feels suffocating. So, I keep walking, my feet carrying me through the familiar streets of the city, my thoughts drifting back to Evie with every step. I wonder what she's thinking right now. I wonder if she's still sitting in the bookstore, replaying everything I said, trying to make sense of it all.

I wish I could take it all back—the lies, the secrets—but I can't. All I can do is hope that what we had before Gareth showed up is still strong enough to survive this.

I walk for hours, the city blurring around me, my mind racing with all the possibilities of what could come next. Maybe Evie will forgive me, and we'll find a way to move forward. Or maybe this is the end. Maybe I've lost her for good.

The uncertainty sits heavy in my chest, but I know I've done all I can. The rest is out of my hands.

As the night wears on, I find myself standing across the street from the bookstore, looking at the warm glow of the lights through the window. Evie's still inside, sitting at the table where we spent so many evenings together. I watch her for a moment, my heart aching with the weight of everything that's happened between us.

I don't go inside. I can't. Not yet.

So I turn and walk away, the cold air biting at my skin, the uncertainty of what comes next hanging over me like a shadow.

And for the first time in a long time, I let go of the control I've been holding onto so tightly.

21

EVIE

The sun slips through the curtains, casting soft rays across my bed, but I don't move. I've been awake for hours, lying here in this half-light, staring at the ceiling, my mind restless and full of thoughts I can't seem to quiet. It's been days—days since Sasha walked out of the bookstore, since she left me sitting at that table with all the shattered pieces of what we used to be.

And I haven't reached out.

I know why. I keep telling myself the same thing, over and over: *I can't go back to her. I can't be the one to break first.* It's a block I can't shake, a wall that's been there for as long as I can remember. My mom was the same way—leaving and never returning. She'd drift in and out of my life like a ghost, and every time I'd reach out, she'd be gone again. Always gone. I learned early on not to be the one who goes looking. You get hurt that way.

But with Sasha, it feels different. Or maybe that's what I want to believe. I don't know anymore.

I close my eyes, but it's worse. All I see is her. Her skin against mine, the feel of her breath on my neck, her fingers tangled in my hair as she whispers my name. I remember the way she made me feel, like I was the only thing in the world that mattered. The way she'd kiss me slowly, taking her time, like she was memorizing every inch of me. I remember the weight of her body pressed against mine, the way we fit together so perfectly in those quiet, intimate moments.

I can still feel her hands on me, the way they'd slide down my sides, rough and soft all at once, between my legs, fingers pushing deep inside of me, leaving trails of heat that would linger long after she was gone. The memory is too real, too vivid. It's like she's still here, but she's not. She's out there somewhere, and I'm lying here, wanting her. Needing her.

But I can't reach out. I just...can't.

It's a mental block I can't get past. The fear is too big, too loud. What if I let her back in, and she leaves again? What if I open up, and she walks away, just like my mom always did? That kind of hurt—I've felt it too many times. I don't think I can survive it again.

Still, every night when I lie here alone in my bed, I find myself wishing she'd come back. Wishing she'd just show up, even though I know it's not fair to hope for that when I'm not willing to make the first move.

∽

The next morning, I drag myself out of bed, though my body feels heavy, like it's weighed down by something invisible. I head to the coffee shop on the corner, the one Sasha and I used to go to. It's become a habit, sitting here, replaying our conversations in my mind. Every corner of this place reminds me of her, and I sit at the table by the window where we used to sit, arguing about poetry or laughing at something absurd. The seat across from me feels empty in a way that nothing can fill.

I can hear her voice, the way she'd tease me, always a little sharp, a little sweet. We'd debate everything—our favorite poets, the best cities in the world, whether iced coffee was superior to hot. She'd argue passionately, her eyes lighting up, and even when we disagreed, there was always that tension between us. The good kind. The kind that made me want to kiss her, just to stop her talking, just to feel her smile against my lips.

I take a sip of my coffee, but it doesn't taste the same. Nothing does.

I keep going over everything she said the last time we spoke. Her apology, the way her voice broke when she admitted why she didn't tell me about Gareth. I understand now, I really do. She was scared, just like I am. Scared of losing something that mattered, scared of being judged for her past. And deep down, I know I've already forgiven her. I forgave her the moment she left the bookstore.

But forgiveness doesn't mean I can reach out. It doesn't mean I can push past the fear that's been sitting in my chest, hard and unmoving, since the day she told me the truth. Because forgiveness is one thing, but trusting her again... that's something else entirely.

And yet, here I am, every day, hoping she'll come back. Wishing she'd walk through the door of this coffee shop or the bookstore, like nothing ever happened. I want her to fight for us, to prove to me that she's not going to disappear. That I can trust her not to leave.

But maybe that's unfair. Maybe I'm asking for too much.

The days blur together, each one a repeat of the last. I go to the bookstore, I shelve books, I help customers, but my mind is always somewhere else. Always on Sasha. Every night, I lie awake, thinking about her, waiting for something to change. Waiting for her to come back. But she doesn't.

It's late afternoon when the bell above the door rings. I'm behind the counter, lost in thought, flipping through the pages of a book I've read a hundred times. I look up, half-expecting another regular customer, but it's not.

It's Glass.

He steps inside, his usual swagger toned down, his expression serious in a way I'm not used to seeing. He looks around the bookstore, his sharp eyes taking in the familiar space before landing on me.

"Well, look who's still hiding," he says, his voice light, but there's an edge to it. He walks over to the counter, resting his hands on it as he looks me over. "You look like hell, Evie."

I raise an eyebrow, trying to muster some kind of defense. "Nice to see you too, Glass."

He shrugs, but there's no humor in his eyes. "You know why I'm here."

I glance down at the counter, suddenly feeling exposed. "If this is about Sasha—"

"Of course it's about Sasha," he interrupts, his tone sharp but not unkind. "She's a mess, you're a mess, and I'm getting tired of watching the two of you dance around each other like this."

I swallow hard, feeling a lump form in my throat. "It's not that simple."

Glass sighs, leaning in a little closer. "I know it's not simple. I'm not saying it is. But what are you waiting for, Evie? She laid everything out for you. She was honest,

The Words of Us

finally. And you're sitting here, what? Wishing she'd come back? Hoping she'll fix this?"

I don't answer. I don't need to. He knows.

"Look, I get it," he continues, his voice softer now. "You've been hurt before. You've got your reasons for not reaching out. But Sasha's not your mom. She's not going to leave you the way your mom did. And you know that."

I flinch at the mention of my mom, the old wound still too raw. "I *don't* know that."

"Yes, you do," he says firmly. "You know her. You know she's not going to just walk away from this unless you make her believe there's nothing left to fight for."

I blink back the tears that are threatening to fall. "I've already forgiven her, Glass. I understand why she didn't tell me. I get it. But I can't—" My voice cracks, and I take a deep breath, trying to steady myself. "I can't reach out. I can't be the one to do it."

He nods slowly, like he expected that answer. "You're scared. I get it. But here's the thing: You don't have to be the one to fix everything. You just need to let her know that you're willing to try. She's out there, Evie. She's waiting for you to give her a sign. Any sign."

I look away, unable to meet his gaze. "What if it's too late?"

Glass gives me a sad smile. "It's only too late if you let it be."

We stand in silence for a long moment, the weight of his words sinking in. I know he's right. Deep down, I know that if I don't do something, I'm going to lose her. Maybe I already have. But the fear, it's still there, gnawing at me, keeping me from reaching out.

"Do you love her?" Glass asks, his voice gentle now.

I don't even hesitate. "Yes."

"Then what are you waiting for?"

I don't have an answer. I don't have anything.

All I have is the hope that maybe, just maybe, it's not too late.

∼

I clutch my journal so tightly my knuckles are white, the worn leather cool against my clammy hands. My heart's been racing since I woke up this morning, and it hasn't slowed down. It won't. Not until I know whether or not she's coming. Whether or not *they're* coming.

The bookstore is already filling up, people drifting in with their conversations and laughter, the familiar clatter of chairs being set up for the night. It's a Saturday, so it's busier than usual, with the usual mix of regulars and curious newcomers who heard about our poetry nights. But tonight is different. Tonight, I'm not just the host. I'm the one waiting to read.

And I'm waiting for *her*.

Glass had said he'd get her here. We'd planned it all out, how he'd bring her to the poetry night, not tell her I'd be reading, just...nudge her in the right direction. He seemed so sure, so confident. But now, as I glance toward the door for what feels like the hundredth time, they're still not here, and doubts start creeping in.

Maybe he couldn't do it. Maybe she said no.

My stomach twists with anxiety, and I take a deep breath, trying to calm myself. It's no use. My mind keeps spinning with possibilities, with all the ways this could go wrong. If she's not here, then what was the point? I'm about to bare my soul, to read something I've never shared with anyone, and I can't even be sure she'll hear it.

The clock ticks closer to the start of the event, and I force myself to focus on the tasks at hand—setting up the microphone, adjusting the chairs, checking the sound system. It's all muscle memory at this point, the routines I've done a thousand times before, but tonight they feel different. Heavier.

I glance at the door again, my heart lurching every time it swings open, but it's never them. People are filing in, taking their seats, but there's still no sign of Glass or Sasha. A knot tightens in my chest, and I feel another pang of doubt creeping in.

Maybe she doesn't want to come. Maybe she doesn't want to see me.

I shake my head, pushing the thought away. Glass promised. He said he'd talk to her, that he'd get her here. But now, with every passing minute, I feel that hope slipping away.

The room buzzes with chatter, people mingling, flipping through poetry books, but all I can hear is the pounding of my heart. I look down at my journal, the one I've been holding like a lifeline, and my stomach flips. I'm not used to this. I'm not a performer. I've hosted these nights for years, but I've never gotten up on that stage and read anything I've written.

But tonight, I'm doing it. I'm doing it for her.

The lights dim slightly, signaling that we're about to start, and I feel a rush of nerves wash over me. I glance at the door one last time, hoping—praying—that I'll see Sasha's face in the crowd, but...nothing.

My heart sinks.

Maybe it's better this way, I tell myself. If she's not here, I won't have to face her reaction. But even as I think it, I know it's a lie. I want her here. I want her to hear my words, to understand everything I've been too afraid to say. I want her to know that I've forgiven her, that I've been waiting for her.

But she's not here.

I take a shaky breath as I walk to the small stage at the front of the room, my journal still clutched in my hands. The familiar faces of the crowd blur together as I climb the steps, the light from the overhead bulbs making the room feel warmer than it is. I feel the weight of every eye on me, but all I can think about is the two people who aren't here.

The microphone crackles as I adjust it, and for a moment, I feel like I'm outside my own body watching someone else do this. Someone else with the courage to stand in front of a crowd and read something deeply personal. But then I catch my reflection in the window, and it's me. It's really me.

I open the journal, my hands trembling slightly as I flip to the page I've read a hundred times, rehearsed in the quiet of my apartment, whispered into the dark of sleepless nights.

The room quiets, and I clear my throat, my voice shaky as I speak into the microphone.

"I-I'm not a poet," I start, forcing a small smile. "I've spent years hosting these nights, listening to so many beautiful voices share their words, their hearts. But tonight, I wanted to try something different, so here's something I wrote."

I pause, my fingers gripping the edges of the journal, and I glance at the door one last time. Still nothing.

She's not coming.

I take a deep breath and begin to read.

"Love is not the kind of thing

The Words of Us

That stays where you leave it.
It lingers in empty spaces,
Takes root in all the places
You never thought to look.

Love is not the kind of thing
    That waits for you to be ready.
    It sneaks up on you,
    Soft as a whisper,
    Sharp as a blade.

Love is not the kind of thing
    That forgives easily.
    It remembers the broken promises,
    The things left unsaid,
    And it holds them close
    Like old scars
    That never quite fade.

But love is the kind of thing
    That waits, even when it shouldn't.
    It waits for the words to come,
    For the fear to fade,
    For the walls to crumble.

Love waits because it knows
    That when the time comes,
    When the fear is gone,
    It will still be there,

Waiting.
Always waiting."

The words hang in the air, suspended between me and the silent crowd. I don't know what I expected—applause, maybe? But all I feel is the quiet weight of their attention, the way they're watching me like they're waiting for something more.

I close the journal, my hands still trembling, and step back from the microphone, my heart pounding. I don't look up. I can't. If I do, I'll see the empty space where I wanted Sasha to be, and I'm not sure I can handle that.

But then the door creaks open.

I glance up, my heart stuttering in my chest.

Sasha.

She's standing in the doorway, her eyes wide, searching the room until they land on me. And behind her, just barely visible, is Glass, giving me a small smile.

I freeze, my breath catching in my throat. She's here. She came.

For a moment, everything else fades away—the room, the crowd, the noise—and it's just us. Just me and Sasha, standing on opposite sides of the room, both of us waiting for the other to make a move.

She hesitates, and then, slowly, she steps forward.

And my heart, the one I thought had been locked up for good, starts to beat again.

EPILOGUE
SASHA 5 YEARS LATER

It's early, and the city is still quiet. I can hear the soft hum of traffic outside the window, the occasional bark of a dog, but inside our little apartment, it's peaceful. The air smells like coffee and books—Evie's doing, of course. She's always got something brewing, whether it's a new blend or a new stack of poetry anthologies spread across the kitchen table.

Our beautiful grey cat, Bruce, stretches himself out and then resettles himself on the window ledge.

I'm lying in bed, watching her move through the room, dressed in one of my old shirts, her hair still a little wild from sleep. It's funny how after all these years, just seeing her like this—comfortable, relaxed, completely herself—can make my heart race.

It's been five years since I almost lost her. Five years since I walked into that bookstore, terrified that it might be the last time I'd see her. And now, here we are, sharing mornings like this. It's still a little surreal.

"You're staring," she says without looking up from her coffee cup, her voice teasing.

"Can you blame me?" I stretch lazily, the sheets cool against my skin. "You're hard to look away from."

She rolls her eyes, but there's a smile tugging at her lips. "Flattery won't get you more coffee."

I laugh, slipping out of bed and padding across the room to stand beside her. I wrap my arms around her waist, pulling her close, and she leans back into me with a soft sigh. It's these little moments, the quiet intimacy of everyday life, that I never take for granted. I spent so long running, hiding from my past, that I never imagined I could have something like this—something that feels so stable, so real.

"Did you finish that poem?" she asks, turning her head slightly to glance at me.

"I'm still working on it," I admit, resting my chin on her shoulder. "It's not...coming out the way I want it to."

"You'll get there," she says softly. "You always do."

I smile against her skin, pressing a kiss to the curve of her neck. "What about you? Have you decided which book to feature for the next poetry night?"

"Not yet." She taps her fingers against the counter, thoughtful. "I was thinking of doing something classic. Maybe Yeats or Auden."

"Always a safe bet," I murmur, tightening my hold on her.

Her breath hitches slightly, and I feel the warmth of her body against mine, the familiar pull of desire sparking between us. Even after all these years, that feeling—the magnetic draw toward her—never fades. It's always there, simmering beneath the surface.

She turns in my arms, her eyes meeting mine, and there's a spark of something in her gaze—something playful, something teasing. "You know, we could have coffee...or we could skip straight to dessert."

I raise an eyebrow, my lips curling into a smirk. "And what kind of dessert are we talking about?"

Her hands slide up my arms, tracing the lines of my muscles, and she leans in, her breath warm against my ear. "The kind that doesn't require leaving the apartment."

God, she knows exactly what she's doing. My body reacts instantly, heat pooling in my stomach, desire thrumming through me like a live wire. I tilt her head back slightly, brushing my lips against hers, but I don't kiss her yet. I want to draw it out, savor the tension.

"You're playing with fire," I whisper, my voice low.

She grins, her fingers tangling in my hair. "I know."

And just like that, the space between us vanishes. My mouth finds hers, the kiss slow at first, but it deepens quickly, heat building between us like it always does. Her hands are in my hair, pulling me closer, and I can't get enough of her. I never can. The taste of her lips, the way her body fits so perfectly against mine—it's intoxicating.

She presses herself closer, and I lift her onto the counter, my hands sliding under the hem of her shirt, feeling the softness of her skin. She gasps into my mouth as my fingers trace up her sides, sending a shiver through her.

"You're supposed to be getting ready for work," I murmur against her lips, though I have no intention of stopping.

She lets out a breathy laugh, her fingers digging into my shoulders. "I think I can be a little late."

I grin, pushing her shirt up over her head, and the sight of her—bare, vulnerable, and mine—makes my pulse race. She pulls me in again, our kisses growing more urgent, more desperate, as the need between us builds. Every touch, every breath, feels electric, and I can't think of anything else but her—how much I want her, how much I love her.

We don't make it to the bedroom.

I don't know how we ended up here, in the hallway, somewhere between the bedroom and the living room, but none of that matters now. All that matters is her—the way she's looking at me, the way her body is trembling under my touch, the way her lips part slightly, like she's waiting for me to take the next step.

I lean in close enough that I can feel her breath on my lips, but I don't kiss her yet. I want to make her wait, to draw this out, to savor the moment before everything else falls away. My fingers trail down her sides, tracing the curve of her hips, and I feel her shudder beneath me.

"Sasha," she whispers, her voice low, needy. "Please…"

Her plea sends a surge of heat through me, and I finally close the distance between us, capturing her lips in a slow, deliberate kiss. It's soft at first, almost gentle, but the hunger is there just beneath the surface, and it doesn't take long for it to rise up, pushing us both over the edge.

Her hands are in my hair, pulling me closer, and I press her harder against the wall, my body flush against hers. I can feel her heart pounding in time with mine, the heat between us growing more intense with every second. I deepen the kiss, my tongue slipping past her lips, tasting her, losing myself in the familiar rhythm of her mouth against mine.

We're moving quickly now, desperate, like we can't get close enough, fast enough. My hands slip under the hem of her shirt, sliding up her smooth skin, and she gasps as my fingers brush the underside of her breasts. I love the way she responds to me, the way her body arches into my touch, the way she's always been so open with me, so willing to give herself over to this.

To us.

I break the kiss just long enough to tug her shirt over her head, tossing it aside carelessly. The cool air hits her skin, and she shivers, her nipples hardening under my gaze. I can't help but smile at the sight of her—so beautiful, so utterly mine.

I drop to my knees in front of her, my hands sliding down her thighs, hooking under the waistband of her panties. I glance up at her, and she's watching me, her eyes dark with desire, her lips parted as she tries to catch her breath.

"Are you sure you want to do this here?" I ask, my voice husky, teasing. "We're not even halfway to the bedroom."

She bites her bottom lip, her fingers tangling in my hair again. "I don't care. Just don't stop."

That's all the encouragement I need.

I tug her underwear down her legs, my lips following the path of my hands, kissing the soft skin of her thighs as I go. She moans softly, her fingers tightening in my hair, and I can feel the tension in her body, the way she's trembling with anticipation.

I pause for a moment, looking up at her and taking in the sight of her standing there. There's something about moments like this—when it's just us, stripped down to nothing but our desire for each other—that makes everything else disappear. It's just her and me, the rest of the world fading into the background.

I press my lips to the inside of her thigh, trailing soft kisses up toward the heat of her pussy, and her breath hitches, her body tensing in anticipation. I can feel her need, the way she's aching for me, and it drives me wild. I want to make her feel everything—every touch, every kiss, every breath.

And then, without another word, I give her what she wants. What we both want.

Her moan echoes through the hallway as I touch her, my fingers exploring her with slow, deliberate movements. Her hips buck against me, her hands gripping my shoulders as she tries to hold on, but I'm not going to let her rush this. I want to take my time, to savor every moment, to make sure she knows just how much I want her.

"Sasha," she breathes, her voice trembling with need. "Please..."

I don't make her beg for long.

I move faster, my fingers slipping inside her and beginning to fuck her, my lips pressing against her clitoris, and the sound she makes—a soft, breathless moan—is enough to send a shiver down my spine. She's so responsive, so completely open to me, and I love the way I can push her to the edge, how I can make her lose herself in this, in us.

She's close now, her body trembling, her breath coming in short, desperate gasps. I can feel her tensing around me, her fingers digging into my shoulders, and I know she's on the verge of falling apart. I push her harder, faster, and when she finally lets go, her release is sudden and explosive, her body arching against me as she cries out my name.

I don't stop, not until she's completely undone, her body trembling in the aftermath. And even then, I hold her close, my lips brushing against her skin as she comes down, my hands steadying her as she leans against the wall for support.

"God, Sasha," she whispers, her voice shaky. "You're going to be the death of me."

I grin, pressing a soft kiss to her lips as I pull her down to the floor, wrapping her up in my arms. We lie there together, tangled in each other, our breathing slowly evening out, the world outside forgotten.

And in this moment, everything feels perfect.

∼

Later, we're lying on the floor, wrapped up in each other, our bodies tangled together in the aftermath of something raw, something powerful. The room is quiet, save for the sound of our breathing, and I feel the weight of her head resting on my chest, her fingers tracing idle patterns on my skin.

"I'm never going to get tired of this," I say quietly, my hand running through her hair.

She hums softly, a contented sound, and I can feel her smile against my skin. "Me neither."

It's moments like this that make me realize how far we've come. There was a time when I didn't think we'd make it—when I thought I'd lose her because of my past, because of the things I was too scared to admit. But she stayed. She forgave me. And together, we built something real.

∼

As the day goes on, the comfort of our routine sets in. We spend the morning in the bookstore, rearranging displays and chatting with customers. It's always busy on Saturdays, and the familiar hum of activity keeps us grounded. The poetry nights have grown over the years, and the bookstore has become more than just a shop—it's a community hub, a place where people come to connect, to share their stories, their art.

Evie thrives here. She's in her element, guiding people to the right books, recommending poems that will change their life. I love watching her work, seeing how effortlessly she moves through this world she's created. And she lets me be a part of it, in the quiet way she always has.

∼

As the afternoon fades into evening, we're back home. The sun is setting, casting a golden light through the windows, and we're curled up on the couch, a bottle of wine between us. The day's been full, but now, it's just us.

We're talking about the future. We do that sometimes—dream about what's next, even though we're both happy with where we are. Evie's been toying with the idea of expanding the bookstore, maybe adding a café or hosting more events, and I've been thinking about starting a poetry workshop for local kids.

"What do you think?" she asks, swirling her wine in her glass. "Should we take the plunge? Go bigger with the bookstore?"

I smile at her, loving the way she gets when she's excited about something. "I think whatever you decide will be the right choice."

She nudges me with her foot. "That's not an answer."

I laugh, leaning over to kiss her cheek. "Fine. I think it's a great idea. The store's already a hit, and you've got the talent to make it even bigger. Plus, it'll give me an excuse to spend more time there."

Her smile softens, and she looks at me for a long moment, something tender in her gaze. "I love you, you know that?"

My heart stutters a little, the warmth of her words settling over me like a blanket. "I love you too."

It's so simple, but it's everything.

∽

Later, we're in bed, the night quiet around us, but I can't sleep. I'm lying on my back, staring at the ceiling, my mind running over the years we've shared and how much we've been through together. I turn to look at her, at the way her face is softened in sleep, her hand resting gently on my chest.

I think about the life we've built. It wasn't easy, not at first. There were times when I wasn't sure if we'd make it, if we'd be able to move past the things that kept us apart. But we did. We found our way back to each other, and now... Now we have this.

I reach out, brushing a strand of hair away from her face, and she stirs, her eyes fluttering open.

"Can't sleep?" she murmurs, her voice soft and sleepy.

"Just thinking," I say quietly, leaning down to press a kiss to her forehead.

"About what?"

"About how lucky I am."

She smiles, her hand sliding up to cup my cheek. "We both are."

I pull her closer, wrapping my arms around her, and she settles against me, her body warm and familiar. We lie there for a long time, the quiet intimacy of the moment wrapping around us like a cocoon.

And as I hold her, I realize that I don't need to think about the future. Because everything I've ever wanted, everything I've ever needed, is right here.

∽

Five years later, and we're still writing our story. Every day, every moment, we add a new line, a new chapter. And I wouldn't change a single word.

The quiet stillness of the night settles over us as I hold her close. Her breathing is soft and even, and for a moment, I just let myself feel it—the warmth of her body against mine, the weight of her arm draped across me. There's something grounding about it, this simple act of being together. It reminds me of how far we've come, how much we've grown since those early days of uncertainty and fear.

I think back to the first time we kissed, to the heat of that moment, and the years of passion and intimacy that followed. Those nights when we couldn't keep our hands off each other, the way we explored each other's bodies with a hunger that seemed to burn forever. But now, there's a different kind of intensity between us—deeper, quieter, more enduring. We still crave each other, but it's balanced by the ease of knowing we're safe in each other's arms.

Her hand moves slightly in her sleep, fingers brushing against my chest, and I can't help but smile. Even in her dreams, she reaches for me.

∼

Kenneth passed away two years ago, and sometimes, I still expect to see him walk through the door of the bookstore, his arms full of new books, his easy smile lighting up the room. He'd been a constant in both our lives, someone who knew the bookstore as intimately as Evie and always seemed to know what we needed before we did. His absence is a quiet ache, a missing piece of the space that can never really be filled. When I walk past the counter, I can almost hear his voice, teasing me about one thing or another, offering unsolicited but always spot-on advice about my latest poem.

After he died, the bookstore felt different for a while—quieter, as if the energy had dimmed. Evie took it hard, of course. He was more than just an employee to her; he was a friend, a confidant, someone who had been by her side during some of her hardest moments. We honored him the best way we knew how: by keeping the poetry nights alive, something he always said was the heart of the place. Now, we always have a moment of silence for Kenneth at the beginning of every big event, and his picture still hangs behind the counter, watching over everything like a silent guardian.

Glass took it hard, too, in his own way. He was never the type to show much emotion, but I could tell it affected him. The four of us were close, bonded by our shared love of words and art, and Kenneth had been the glue that held a lot of things together. After Kenneth's passing, Glass threw himself into his work, performing more and pushing the boundaries of his poetry, almost as if he were trying to outrun the grief. It wasn't until recently that he found a kind of peace with it, and I think that's what led him to where he is now—performing on bigger stages, his voice reaching more people than ever before.

Watching Glass perform these days is something else entirely. There's always been an intensity to him when he's on stage, but now there's a fire that wasn't there before. It's as if losing Kenneth pushed him to dig deeper, to find parts of himself he hadn't tapped into yet. His poetry is sharper, more raw, and audiences respond to him in a way that's electric. He's become something of a local legend, and whenever we watch him perform, I can't help but feel a swell of pride for my friend who's finally stepping into the spotlight he deserves.

Evie and I still keep in touch with him, of course. He comes by the bookstore when he can, and we sit and reminisce about the old days, laughing about Kenneth's terrible taste in coffee and his surprisingly good taste in poetry. But those visits are fewer and farther between now that Glass is performing more often. It's strange to think of him on those bigger stages with audiences hanging on his every word, but he's earned it. I know Kenneth would be proud, too, seeing how far Glass has come since those quiet nights at the bookstore.

In a way, both of them—Kenneth and Glass—are still part of what we do here. The bookstore isn't just about the books or the poetry nights. It's about the community we built, the people we've loved and lost, and the ones who've helped shape us along the way. Even though Kenneth is gone and Glass is out there performing for the world, their spirits are still here, woven into the fabric of everything we do. And for that, I'm endlessly grateful.

~

The next morning, I wake before her, the soft light of dawn spilling through the curtains. I sit up slowly, careful not to disturb her, and slip out of bed. I pause for a moment, watching her sleep, and my chest tightens with love. It's overwhelming sometimes, how much I feel for her. How much I know she's changed my life.

I head into the kitchen and start brewing coffee, the rich scent filling the apartment. It's one of our favorite rituals— mornings spent sipping coffee, reading poetry, talking about everything and nothing. The kind of mornings I never thought I'd have with anyone, let alone with someone like Evie. Someone who saw through all my walls and chose to stay.

As the coffee drips, I wander over to the window and look out at the city. New Orleans is waking up, the streets slowly coming to life. I love this city—the energy, the people, the way it feels like home. But what I love most is that it's where we found each other.

Evie joins me a few minutes later, her hair a little messy from sleep, one of my shirts hanging loosely off her shoulder. She smiles at me, that soft, lazy smile that always makes my heart skip a beat.

"Morning," she says, her voice still husky from sleep.

"Morning," I reply, handing her a cup of coffee.

She takes a sip, closing her eyes in appreciation. "Perfect as always."

We settle onto the couch, the quiet of the morning stretching out between us. It's comfortable, this silence, and I feel a sense of peace that I never thought I'd have. We don't need to fill the space with words; we've reached a point where just being together is enough.

But after a while, Evie sets her cup down and looks at me, her expression thoughtful. "I've been thinking," she says slowly, her eyes meeting mine.

"Oh?" I raise an eyebrow, curious. "About what?"

"About the bookstore. About us. About what's next."

I nod, leaning back into the cushions. "Go on."

"I've been wondering if maybe we should do more with the poetry nights, maybe even start publishing some of the work that comes out of them. We could turn the bookstore into a real hub for the community. What do you think?"

I consider her words, a smile tugging at my lips. "I think

it's a brilliant idea. You've built something amazing there, and I'd love to see it grow."

Her face lights up with excitement, and she leans forward, her eyes sparkling. "You really think we could do it?"

"I know we can," I say, reaching out to take her hand. "We're a good team, remember?"

She smiles, squeezing my hand. "We really are, aren't we?"

~

As the day goes on, we work on plans for the bookstore, jotting down ideas and brainstorming how we could turn our little shop into something even bigger. The excitement is palpable between us, and I love seeing her so passionate about this. She's always been the heart of the bookstore, and now she wants to share that heart with even more people.

Later, after the plans have been made and the excitement has settled, we find ourselves curled up on the couch again, this time with a bottle of wine and soft music playing in the background. The sun has set, and the apartment is bathed in the warm glow of lamplight.

Evie's head rests on my shoulder, and I run my fingers through her hair, feeling the familiar pull of desire building between us. It's a different kind of desire now—more mature, more grounded in the life we've built together. But it's no less intense.

I tilt her chin up, brushing a kiss against her lips. "You know," I murmur, my voice low, "I'm still not tired of you."

She smiles against my mouth, her fingers tracing the line of my jaw. "Good. Because I'm definitely not tired of you."

I deepen the kiss, letting it linger, savoring the taste of

her. Her hands move to my waist, tugging me closer, and the heat between us grows. It's a slow burn, the kind that comes from knowing each other inside and out, from years of trust and love. Every touch feels like a promise, every kiss a reminder of how far we've come.

We don't rush. There's no need to. We have all the time in the world.

~

Later, we lie tangled together in the sheets, the night quiet around us. Evie is draped across me, her head resting on my chest, her breath slow and even. My hand moves in lazy circles on her back, and I feel a deep sense of contentment settle over me.

"I love you," she whispers, her voice soft in the darkness.

"I love you too," I reply, pressing a kiss to the top of her head.

She shifts slightly, looking up at me with those eyes that always manage to steal my breath. "Do you think we've made it?"

I smile, my heart swelling with affection. "Yeah, I think we have."

We've built a life together—a life full of love, trust, and understanding. It wasn't always easy, but it was always worth it. And now, as I hold her close, I know that we'll keep writing our story, one day at a time.

Because this? This is what I've always been waiting for.

And I'm never letting it go.

AFTERWORD

Thank you so much for reading this one. Evie and Sasha are very close to my heart. I spent many years of my own life running away and keeping secrets like Sasha and being able to give Sasha her happy ever after meant the world to me.

∼

If you enjoy this series, why don't you check out my Secret Love series?

Is losing yourself in the bed of a seductive and beautiful stranger the best way to solve your problems?

This is an Age Gap Romance set on the beautiful coastline of Spain. It is hot and steamy in nature (you have been warned!)

Haley Anderson has run away to Spain following the breakdown of her marriage. She wants to start again, to find something, to find herself perhaps.

She doesn't expect to be swept off her feet and into the bed of a beautiful older woman.

What secrets is this woman hiding? And will Haley be able to find herself in the arms of someone else?

getbook.at/Haley

FREE BOOK

Pick up my book, Summer Love for FREE when you sign up to my mailing list.

On a beach in France, Summer crashes into Max's life and changes everything. This is a hot and heady summer romance. https://BookHip.com/MFPGZAX

My mailing list is the best place to be the first to find out about new releases, Free books, special offers and price drops. You'll also find out a bit about my life and the inspiration behind the stories and the characters. Oh, and you'll love Summer Love. :)

Printed in Great Britain
by Amazon